THE FALSE
PROPHET

A Novel by
Destiny

To submit a manuscript for our review,

email us at

submissions@majorkeypublishing.com

Chapter 1

Peace Temple was packed that Sunday morning. A guest speaker, Bishop McConnell, was bringing "The Word," and Faith had been waiting to see him in person for months. She followed his podcast and read a few of his books. Beside him was his elegant wife that wore a white suit with a gold sash tied around her neck. She looked like royalty. The way First Lady McConnell sat upright and looked her husband in the eye when he mentioned her name pulled on Faith's heartstrings. At forty-years old, she had yet to have a man look at her the way Bishop McConnell looked at his wife. She had experienced relationships before in the past, but they never lasted beyond two years. She had met so many men that promised her the world, but her ring finger was left bare every time.

Faith had been trying to find "Mr. Right" in church

for years. Her friends warned her that he wouldn't be there, but she couldn't imagine getting comfortable with someone who didn't walk and talk God's word. Her eyes had been set on a pastor since as far back as she could remember. However, she was willing to settle for a traveling minister without a church or even a deacon. Every church she visited had more single women than she could count. There were plenty of married men and the single men were too old or recently divorced.

This time, she had come to church to find a man. She wanted to hear God's word too and she knew Bishop McConnell was very popular with young men. Unlike most Bishops that attracted single mothers and elderly women, Bishop McConnell's books and speaking engagements were attended by majority men. He taught lessons on fatherhood, being a husband, and taking on leadership roles in the church and the community.

Faith expected the turnout to have nothing but raging testosterone in every crevice of the church but instead hundreds of women filled every bench in Peace Temple. From single mothers to grandmothers that hated being in the midst of young people that weren't their own.

Her plan had failed miserably but she had a glimmer of hope that some lonely, handsome man would walk in and sit on a pew much further back from her and wink. That's how it was in the movies and that's how her friends described meeting their men. It was supposed to be sudden. You were supposed to be in the right place at the right time. Her heart was supposed to start beating like a drum the moment she saw him. The heavens would open up and then her prince would take her hand and ask her to come into his life as the virginal, Christian woman he was waiting for.

But that dream never came into fruition. She was getting older and the chance that a single man in his forties with no children who was willing to wait until marriage to have sex was as slim as winning the California Powerball.

Bishop McConnell spoke of the fading of the strong Black family both in everyday life and in the media. He stressed how important it was for young women to wait for a God-fearing man that wanted to lead their family. With his booming, baritone voice the women in the building were all on the edge of their seats as if they were listening for their names to be called. Hundreds of women and men stood to their feet in response to his words. Faith shed a tear.

"You know, a lot of women's problem these days is that they're looking for the wrong man! A lot of y'all women want to turn these thugs into husbands, and it ain't gonna work! Look like a Christian woman. Carry yourself like a Christian woman. Carry yourself like someone's wife and I guarantee that the man God has made for you will be right around the corner."

Faith stood with a tear in her eye and focused on the Bishop's words. An emptiness settled in her heart while she reflected upon her own life. She had lived the most

Christian life she could. She was still a virgin and never gave "thugs" the time of day. She made herself available in the church by getting on committees and even going by herself for lunch during the weekend hoping to meet someone new. She had read all the Christian dating books and had even gone to dating seminars. Nothing worked. There were a plethora of men but few of them claimed to be saved.

Faith stayed until the end of service. At benediction, she slowly grabbed her purse and Bible. While walking toward the exit, she saw a dark-skinned man with dimples who she had never seen before. Faith never liked to approach men but he seemed friendly and wasn't talking to anyone yet.

She made a beeline toward him but was only about two feet away when she saw a woman grab his hand. He squeezed it and kissed the woman on the forehead. A little boy, that looked just like him, raised his arms toward the Denzel Washington lookalike and cried, "daddy."

The walk back to the car was a quick one. She didn't care to make too much conversation with her closest church friends. It was going to be another teary-eyed drive home. Faith could barely contain her emotions when she put her car in drive.

She played classical music from her cellphone into her Bluetooth to calm her but her vision became blurry with each falling tear. There had been dozens of other very single women just like her at church. There were women like her everywhere she went. Unfortunately, she was the oldest woman she knew that was still single. Her best friend met her husband at thirty-five. That was typically the age when women usually began to panic when they hadn't found the one. Faith had begun to feel nervous about her future in her thirties but she refused to marry an unsaved, bartender like her friend, Tara, married.

She wasn't that desperate then. But now, she regretted the fact that she could have led a man into the church instead of looking for him there.

Tara's husband had begun to go to church more often and had even gotten baptized since they got married. Although her friend worried about her fertility, she gave birth to a healthy baby boy at thirty-seven.

Although she was elated for her friend and growing family, she could feel small twinges of jealousy every time Tara gushed about her husband and two-year-old. Tara had just announced that she was expecting another child soon. It hurt Faith to be jealous of anyone because she knew that feeling was un-Christian but she had done everything right and still didn't get the man she prayed for. Tara and several other women she had remained friends with over the years had given up their virginity long ago. Tara had had sex with at least five men once she left college. She never judged her but Faith appreciated how none of her friends judged her to remain a virgin until marriage. The only people that ever had a problem with her decision were the men she dated. She attempted long distance relationships, which ended up being her longest romances, but they eventually fizzled out once they knew that she was serious about waiting for the ring.

Faith arrived at her apartment fifteen minutes later. She had never left the South Los Angeles neighborhood where she grew up. Demographically, it had many more Hispanic residents and many of the black men she had grown up with had moved out of state or seventy miles away into the cheaper parts of the desert. The violence around her was nothing like it used to be in the nineties, but she came home to the police in front of her building talking to an elderly Hispanic lady known as Maria Guadalupe. Faith already knew it had something to do with the woman's granddaughter and her abusive boyfriend. They were always arguing. Faith didn't understand why the girl wouldn't leave and why the grandmother wouldn't just kick the young man out. They caused the most ruckus in the whole neighborhood. Faith prayed daily that God would move them out somewhere else.

Her apartment faced Downtown Los Angeles. She could see the skyscrapers tower over the city on a beautiful clear day. Los Angeles had been the city of dreams for so many. It was the ultimate land of opportunity. Faith had been able to find a steady job as a school administrative assistant. She had done some print modeling in her twenties, and her church choir had received a multitude of opportunities by being located in Los Angeles. She had gotten the chance to travel all over the country with her voice.

Yet, with her church clothes strewn across her desk chair, she held herself in a fetal position, looking at the other side of the bed. Who would she come home to one day? Who would stare into her eyes like Bishop McConnell looked at his wife?

A single tear soaked into her pillow and she breathed out a deep sigh. She clutched her pillow in an attempt to imagine what it would be like to hold a man in her arms. She had never considered herself desperate before but she had to admit that she was on the brink of full blown depression caused by loneliness. It was a hole that friendships, her job, her family, or even her dog, Sprinkles, would never be able to fill.

Then her phone began to vibrate.

It was her mother. Faith sighed but took the call. She needed to talk about anything other than the self-defeatist thoughts running through her head.

"Hello?" Faith said weakly.

"What's wrong with you?" Her mother said in her naturally shrill voice.

"Is it really that bad that I'm still single? I feel like God is skipping over me to go to everybody else."

"Oh, Faith. I named you Faith! Looks like you don't have any right now."

"How much faith can muster right now at forty with no husband and no kids?"

"You were busy working and didn't you say you wanted to be a world missionary and travel to Haiti to work with their children?"

"I also wanted my own children, Mother. I make myself available and the men are either taken or not Christian."

"Faith, ever since you were a child I always envisioned you as a first lady of a church. I haven't given that up. You are never too old to marry."

"What about children?"

"You can always adopt."

"Mother, I'm most likely sitting on my last eggs."

"You're so dramatic, Faith. Well, I don't know. How do young people find each other these days?" Her mother chuckled.

"I'm not exactly a spring chicken," Faith chuckled.

"That's true, but maybe you should be more open to other races, men who are shorter than six feet, and someone who doesn't make as much as you but has a good job."

Faith wanted to end the call that moment and let out a loud groan but she remembered that her mother could still slap her if she wanted to.

"Mother, the Lord told me that I am going to get everything I want and need in a husband. I don't have to start lowering my standards in desperation."

"Well you sound desperate to tell you the truth. When I met your father, I wasn't so picky."

"I see women on social media find tall, handsome, saved husbands all the time. It can be done."

"You don't know those people and stop comparing your life to others. You don't know the dynamics of their relationship. You're looking at a picture. The man could be beating his wife every day but you're up here looking at some picture. Young folk these days I tell ya." Her mother sighed.

"Well thanks for cheering me up, Mother." Faith said rolling her eyes harder than she had done in a while.

"I got something on the stove, I'll call you back," Faith said, opening her laptop. She checked her emails and began closing tabs while her mother gave her a long-winded rebuke.

Faith finally cut her off and ended the call. She searched for African American Christian dating sites and signed up for the first two she came across. She then downloaded a Black singles app on her phone. Online dating was supposed to be her last resort. She assumed only unattractive women used dating apps. She had always been compared to Kelly Rowland when she was younger but with a heavier bottom half and slightly lighter eyes. Men flocked to her while she was young but once they found out she was a conservative Christian that refused to have sex before walking down the aisle, all the men she met eventually disappeared into thin air.

One of the dating sites required a subscription so she got out her credit card and took a deep breath. It was highly rated online and she had heard a couple of friends use it for dates. She had never heard of anyone actually meeting someone that was marriage material on there. Unfortunately, she had visited every church in her area. She had even attended church conferences in hopes of meeting a bachelor. She had officially exhausted all her options.

Filling out the application felt like she was giving up a part of her soul. It felt shameful but, by the time she completed it, her excitement increased.

Right in front of her for the first time in a long time,

were eligible Christian Black men that came from all walks of life.

She didn't want to message anyone but she sent virtual "winks" to the men that she had interest in. It was like being in the middle of a candy store with access to your parent's entire wallet while they shopped somewhere else.

After an hour passed, Faith was still locked in. She couldn't believe that she had wasted so much time on a website. As she studied the profile, her heart became much heavier.

Many of the men were divorced with young children. Some had never been married but still had children. Faith wanted someone with no young children. She had heard horror stories of ladies she had known in the past that had their relationship attacked with baby momma drama.

The men weren't as handsome as she would have liked. Her filter for her age range resulted in men that were too far away and she was not interested in a long-distance relationship.

Her hands began to cramp two hours later. She had turned on some music and ordered some food to continue her search on her couch.

She almost jumped off her couch when she heard an alert for her messages. Finally, God was at least turning the wheels. She opened it. The picture appeared to be from a professional man with a bald head and a wide, friendly grin. His profile appeared to completely match hers and he even identified as Pentecostal.

Ay, u cute. Wat church u go 2. U got kids. I just got out n im lukin for a new strt. Hit me if u interest.

Faith abruptly closed her laptop and didn't open it again that night or the next.

❖

"Girl, are you really going? You just not gonna give up, huh?" Tara laughed.

Faith and Tara had been best friends since elementary school but Tara had always been more interested in settling down early. She was married with another baby on the way and had encouraged her husband to come to church more often. Faith was happy with her friend but she felt that God had more in store for her. She was certain that God would bless her with a husband that already had some strong ties to a church.

"Yes, I saw a flier for it at church." Faith said, smoothing her skirt. She sprayed on her favorite Dior perfume and checked her edges to make sure they were as smooth as yesterday. She had just gotten her hair pressed. Faith figured that "saved" men liked women that wore their hair straight and long. She felt her naturally curly hair might make her appear too wild.

"A flier for lay members? I thought it was for potential pastors and missionaries?"

"I'm going to get more information on how to be a certified missionary."

"Girl, you going there to find out how to get a certified man. Don't play."

"If I meet him there, then God is good. I'm not going just to meet somebody."

"Faith, you know you're going to look around and try to find out where all the single men are sitting. You don't have to be desperate."

Faith felt the blood in her veins freeze. Her best friend's words began to make her hands shake. "Desperate? Wow, I didn't think you'd ever say something like that about me. I'm using my resources to meet more like-minded people. If I find my husband there, then so be it."

"Faith, I just want you to just relax. You can date but it's not a race."

"That's so easy for you to say, Tara. You found your man and got your baby. I just hit forty and have little to show for it."

"You have life, health, and strength, Faith. You also have a good job, your own place, and a car. You have plenty to show for. You're like one of the pillars of Peace Temple. They rely on you for everything. I don't know a committee you're not on."

"Tara, you'll never know what it's like to live each day knowing you should have had a family by now. It hurts."

Faith could tell Tara was still trying to find words

to say but instead just cleared her throat and sighed. "Just be careful, girl."

Her new stilettos scraped against her wood floor as she tried to grab her jean jacket just in case the air conditioning was too cool inside the banquet room. She had a tight-fitting gold dress that hugged her small waist and squeezed around her butt and hips. It flared on the hem that touched her lower legs. She had just purchased a curling wand to slightly bend the ends of her hair.

The event was called the "Up and Coming Pastors' and Missionaries' Luncheon" that was held at a hotel in Long Beach by the water.

Once she arrived, the valet was steadily helping men and women out of their luxury vehicles. Faith had never seen so many BMWs and Teslas in one place. She parked her 2014 Camry in the parking lot and made sure she kept her ticket in her purse so she could get it validated.

Almost at once, dozens of sharply dressed young pastors passed by. Some of them wore the clergy and others wore long gold crosses that swung as they walked. She followed them to the main banquet room where hundreds of men and women were trying to find their seats. She had purchased a seat at a table closer to the podium for the main speaker. There would be praise dancing, instrumental music, a light lunch, and a raffle.

There were other tables that had light refreshments such as cake and cookies. Faith kept to herself and meekly smiled at the other men and women at her table. She planned on telling everyone around her that she was working on being licensed as a missionary if they asked.

None of the women at her table seemed friendly. They all wore large church hats with a variety of feathers and beads. The men at the table were older, arrogant, and unattractive. They were all dressed nice but she was still praying on having a husband that didn't have a receding hairline.

The music began five minutes later and the murmuring amongst the audience reduced. Faith was hoping her adventure wasn't a waste of time. She scanned the room and saw a few men that caught her eyes but none caught hers.

The first speaker, Bishop Jedson, stood up to say the opening prayer. He then began with acknowledgements of the special guest speakers and then took his seat. Lunch was served immediately while soft Gospel music was played by the musicians in the corner.

How is it?

Faith received a text from Tara.

It's fine. I'm enjoying myself. She lied.

She attempted to make conversation with the lady sitting next to her that had on all red. The *White Diamonds* perfume she wore tickled Faith's throat every time she opened her mouth so she ended their interaction early.

Looking around, Faith decided to stand and give a few people a glimpse of her outfit. She didn't mean to wear it behind a table all afternoon.

Tossing her hair behind her as she grabbed a chocolate chip cookie to put on a small plate, someone else had decided they wanted that item too. Long, thin masculine fingers brushed against hers. She didn't know what it felt like to be electrocuted, but when her eyes met his, she was sure that the instant heat in her body had been caused by his touch.

"Well it looks like we're reaching for the same cookie. Should we play rock, paper, scissors?" The man chuckled. His deep, velvety voice reverberated in her ears.

Faith didn't know what to say but allowed herself to smile and then look down.

"My name Blake McPherson," he said reaching out

subject to Maryland Lottery regulations and State Law. The Maryland Lottery is not liable for tickets or prizes previously claimed.

TO CLAIM A PRIZE: Present this ticket to any Maryland Lottery retailer. Validated winning tickets valued up to $600 are eligible for INSTANT PAYOFF. Validated winning tickets valued higher than $600 will be paid after claim is filed. Void if mutilated, altered, or irregular in any manner. Visit the Lottery website at mdlottery.com for locations to claim prizes over $600.

Name

Signature

Tickets are heat sensitive. Do not expose to prolonged periods of excessive heat or light.
Visit the Lottery website at mdlottery.com ®
Rev. 9/20/2017

67624077

IMPORTANT INFORMATION: PLEASE SIGN THE BACK OF YOUR TICKET. This ticket is a bearer instrument. Anyone possessing a winning ticket may claim the prize. Valid only for date(s) shown. Prizes must be claimed within 182 days of the drawing. All winners, tickets, and transactions are subject to Maryland Lottery regulations and State Law. The Maryland Lottery is not liable for tickets or prizes previously claimed.

TO CLAIM A PRIZE: Present this ticket to any Maryland Lottery retailer. Validated winning tickets valued up to $600 are eligible for INSTANT PAYOFF. Validated winning tickets valued higher than $600 will be paid after claim is filed. Void if mutilated, altered, or irregular in any manner. Visit the Lottery website at mdlottery.com for locations to claim prizes over $600.

Name

Signature

Tickets are heat sensitive. Do not expose to prolonged periods of excessive heat or light.
Visit the Lottery website at mdlottery.com ®
Rev. 9/20/2017

67624078

IMPORTANT INFORMATION: PLEASE SIGN THE BACK OF YOUR TICKET. This ticket is a bearer instrument. Anyone possessing a winning ticket may claim the prize. Valid only for date(s) shown. Prizes must be claimed within 182 days of the drawing. All winners, tickets, and transactions are subject to Maryland Lottery regulations and State Law. The Maryland Lottery is not liable for tickets or prizes previously claimed.

MEGA MILLIONS

MARYLAND LOTTERY

1335900402550272221T-71
29 Jul 2022 17:05
Term: 9460103S-01
15e152bd

---

01 06 62 65 66 MB:14 QP

MP:Y   1 Draw - $3.00   07/29

MEGA MILLIONS JACKPOT 07-29-22 $1.28 BILLION Cash $747.2 MIL.

In the month of June we awarded

38,146 COUPONS

SIGN UP. WIN REWARDS.™

MULTI MATCH JACKPOT IS $1,675,000.
LET YOURSELF PLAY!

OP1X K-7BHMN-8K62O-0ZOGG-TFWB1

Scan with My
Lottery Rewards
App.

his hand to shake hers.

"Faith Kerry."

"You're a pastor?" he asked with a slight laugh.

"No, I'm thinking of becoming a missionary. I'm not sure yet. I guess I'm not supposed to be here."

"Why would you say that? Everyone is welcome especially those that are still making up their minds."

Faith carefully placed a chocolate chip cookie on her clear, plastic plate. Blake grabbed another cookie and then placed a few grapes on his plate. He took two steps closer to her and Faith swore she could feel his masculine energy push through her body.

She could tell that he was certainly more than six feet tall. His hair was in carefully brushed waves that reminded her of El Debarge during his peak in the mid-1980s. He had a slimmer build but she could tell that he carefully tailored his suit to fit his body. A dazzling silver watch hung off his wrist. He had a dimple in his right cheek and a closely shaven beard that covered his face. Even his eyebrows were perfect and beautifully framed his warm hazel eyes. He wore a single diamond earring in his right ear. If he hadn't been a stranger, Faith would have fallen into his arms to sample what a kiss from his full, moist lips would feel like.

"Faith, huh? That's a beautiful name. Your parents were saved, huh?"

"They were. My father is a minister and my mother has been a church organist for years."

"I come from a musical family myself. I've been focused on so many other things now, I haven't had the time to explore that talent."

The musicians were done with their piece. It was time for one of the guest speakers to present. Faith didn't want to sit down yet but didn't want Blake to feel as if she was too enamored with him. Looking at him almost caught her up in a daze.

"I guess we should go back to our seats. It looks like someone is about to get up and speak."

"True. What table are you sitting at?"

"Table 5."

"I'm Table 7."

Faith was surprised because she was sure she had scanned the room in that direction. "Well, I thank God for finding a new friend in Christ. I hope this event blesses your journey."

"And yours as well, love."

Faith tugged on her purse that hung on her shoulder and walked slowly to her seat. She was glad she hadn't taken her jacket. She walked slow enough to let her hips sway from side to side. She glanced back at him a few seconds in and he was still staring at her with a half-smile. His dimple partially appeared. He smoothly rubbed his lips together and winked.

Faith prayed that her most feminine walk back to her seat was her sexiest one yet. She thanked herself for making sure that she wore the only dress that revealed both her small waist and round booty at the same time.

During the rest of the event, Faith couldn't maintain her focus anymore. She could feel Blake's eyes on her but she didn't want to make it too obvious that she was also interested.

A heavyset pastor that reminded her of T.D. Jakes shouted, "Tell your neighbor, you will receive everything you ask God for!"

He had just given a long-winded testimony of how working with various ministers in Los Angeles led to a brotherhood that helped him start his first church.

Faith turned around and tried to get the eye contact of the *White Diamonds* perfume lady but Blake's tender smile wound up in her peripheral vision. They caught eyes while he leaned over to his right to repeat the phrase to the man next to him.

Faith felt like a giddy schoolgirl. She couldn't wait for the event to end so she could slip over to his table and possibly get his number. She only knew his first name so it was no point in searching for him on social media.

The speakers seemed to never end. The missionary segment was even longer. There were more singers, a video promoting African missions, and even a chance to be a Sunday School teacher in Haiti for a summer.

Part of her wanted to be able to freely travel around the world and become a missionary in Africa to help introduce Christianity to those who looked like herself. She had seen many of the missions her acquaintances had gone on from Korea to India and she felt that traveling to spread God's word might be her calling. She had planned to take a summer off one year and work with a larger church that was hosting a missionary trip.

However, all of that was before she decided that she needed to get married and have children as soon as humanly possible. Her dream of being someone's wife superseded her need to travel. She could travel at any age but it was scaring her that she was going to be the oldest person she ever knew to get married for the first time.

Faith tiptoed out of the banquet hall in the hotel right before the speaker sat down. She said her "goodbyes" to her table, put her jacket on, and found the nearest exit.

She slowed down hoping Blake was behind her. Once she reached the lobby, she felt someone touch her arm.

"Miss Faith? You were leaving before I got a chance to get to know you?"

Faith abruptly turned her head and let her fingertips

34

brush against his.

"I was wondering if we could exchange numbers. I'm so glad I caught up with you. I saw you trying to sneak out."

His smooth voice faded into a whisper.

Faith took her cellphone out. It almost slipped out of her hands as her fingertips had become suddenly sweaty.

Blake took out his phone and Faith told him her number.

"I'll text you just to give you mine," he said.

"I got it. Thank you."

Blake sent a winking Emoji.

"I hope we can keep in contact. I'm glad I was able

to make another friend in Christ. You prefer to text right?" Faith asked, trying to stop her hands from shaking.

"Actually, I prefer to call. I think texting should be for short messages. I want to hear your voice. Would you mind if I talked to you tonight? If you were busy, we could talk another time."

Faith could smell his cologne linger into her nose. This time, she craved the smell and didn't want to leave where she was standing. "We could talk tonight. I wouldn't mind."

"Then it's settled. I'll call you tonight at eight o'clock."

Faith shook his hand and turned to go back toward her car. She got her parking ticket validated and could barely contain her excitement while she looked for her phone to text Tara.

Girl! You wouldn't believe what just happened?
What?

I got a number. He reminds me of a blend between Drake and El Debarge. He's gorgeous. He's an up and coming pastor. Also, can you believe he would rather call than text? This is a true gentleman.

Now Faith, let the man call first. I'm sure he's a good one.

I'm really sure about this one. I think God is finally moving more for me. Faith texted back while juggling her purse, phone, and keys.

She turned the ignition on in her car and drove slowly out of the parking lot. Part of her wanted to know if she would see him exit the hotel.

Once she gave the parking attendant her ticket, she saw Blake enter his red Tesla with butterfly doors. She saw him tip the driver and then pull his long legs into the driver's seat.

Her heart began stirring inside her chest. She gently bit her lip and continued driving.

By the time she got to the hotel's exit, she noticed Blake had sped up behind her. His car was quiet, so she didn't hear him.

He pulled over next to her and she tried not to look but she eventually turned her gaze toward him and smiled with a closed mouth. She quickly looked away before he could notice what she was doing.

Faith played some of her favorite Gospel tunes on the way home and felt like she was gliding back to her apartment.

When she arrived, she put on some comfortable clothes, turned on some music, cooked a light dinner and waited for her phone to ring. The anticipation was killing her but she knew the wait would be worth it.

Her phone rang at eight o'clock on the dot that evening.

Chapter 2

A couple days later, Faith was still trying to make sure she hadn't been dreaming all of it up. Blake had called her on time as promised the other day and neither one wanted to get off the phone at 11 P.M. Faith had completely thrown out the rule her mother told her, when she was younger, that a man should never end the conversation first. Faith had simply forgotten she was talking to someone she had just met.

They had so much in common. They both grew up in church. Blake had gotten saved, sanctified, and filled with the Holy Ghost at twelve years old like she did. They had both been baptized at thirteen by their pastor grandfathers. Neither of them knew what it was like to go an entire week without going to church at least three times.

Faith and Blake knew what it was like to have to do homework while on the pews of the church during Bible study. They were both spanked as children if they failed to memorize The Lord's Prayer.

Blake felt like a kindred soul. The conversation was easygoing. It didn't feel like she had to find things to talk about. She could also tell that Blake was a good listener. Many men that she spoke to on the phone loved to talk more about themselves especially in Los Angeles. Known as one of the hardest cities to date in, men in L.A. were usually too busy bragging about who they knew and what they supposedly did in the entertainment industry.

Since their phone call, Blake and Faith had been texting every day. She always received a "Good Morning" and "Good Afternoon" text that helped to make her busy mornings and exhausted evenings worthwhile.

When she arrived at her job at King Middle School, her coworkers already noticed something different about her.

"What you smiling so hard about?" Irma, the Dean's assistant, said.

"Nothing. I'm just happy to be up this morning. The week is almost over."

"Girl, it's just Wednesday. Are you okay?"

"I think she's talking to somebody," Martha, the attendance counselor said.

Faith looked around and lowered her voice. "Okay, I just met someone."

Irma and Martha were her closest work friends so both got out of their office chairs and rushed over to her like two excited puppies.

They began asking several questions at once.

"I met him at a church event. He's just lovely. He's truly the most wonderful man I ever met. He's saved and living for Christ and a pastor."

"A pastor?" Irma asked. "See, I always told Martha you were gonna be a pastor's wife."

"Well, we haven't had the marriage talk yet but I'm sure it's coming soon. I mean, this one seems like he wants to settle down. Also, he talks on the phone and not just text."

"Did he ask you out on a date?" Martha asked.

Faith and Blake had planned to go out to dinner on Friday night. She had ordered a new dress online that would match some new shoes she bought two weeks ago. Her hair appointment was Thursday night after church and she was supposed to skip the first half of the work day to get her nails done.

"He did. We're going to Fontellini's in Santa Monica. It's a really nice Italian restaurant."

"I've heard of it. Good choice," Irma commented. "Now how does he look? You got a picture?"

Faith pulled up his picture on her social media. She had just begun to follow him and adored how his social media presence matched how he behaved in real life. Every Sunday, he made a live video where he prayed for people and interpreted Bible scriptures. She noticed that he had at least one hundred people watching at one time. He wanted to start his own church soon and some of his twenty-five thousand followers who lived in the area were very supportive.

"He kind of reminds me of El Debarge," Martha said. "He has some beautiful hair."

"I thought he looked like Drake because he's tall and has a really nice body. I can tell he goes to the gym often. He actually inspires me to get back in the gym."

Faith said scrolling through his pictures on his page.

"Well, this is the happiest I've seen you in a while," Irma said touching Faith's shoulder. "He appears to be a very nice man. How old is he?"

"My age. He looks younger but we were born the same year."

Throughout the rest of the day, Faith could barely keep her focus on the work she needed to complete in the office. It was as if everything was spinning around her but she was floating from one minute to the next with Blake on her mind.

He texted her suddenly around lunchtime.

How's my sweetheart doing? I can't wait to see you on Friday.

I can't wait to see you too. Luckily, I have your

social media page to tide me over.

Let me show you some pictures that I haven't put on there. Blake replied.

Instantly, he sent her pictures of himself shirtless and with a sweaty tank top on. He squinted his eyes in the pictures and lightly but his lip. A single curl fell on his forehead in a gym selfie. Faith could tell he knew he was handsome but she adored when men had confidence.

A little piece of her wondered how someone as handsome as him was so into her. She would have assumed that he would have been arrogant and only wanted to be with someone who looked and dressed like Beyoncé every day.

Faith decided to do her own nails on Friday morning, so she didn't have to take off work for half a day; but when she was finally off at four, she couldn't get home fast enough. Her heart refused to stop pounding until she got a confirmation text that he would be over her place to pick her up in an hour.

While fussing with her curls in the mirror, Faith received a text from Blake.

What are you wearing?

A simple black dress. I'm wearing a cropped, silver jacket with it.

How short is it?

Faith was slightly taken aback. **Um, it's not too short.**

You don't have on all that make-up do you? I love a natural face.

Faith checked in the mirror to see how much she had put on. She was wearing false eyelashes, foundation, eyeliner, deep burgundy lipstick, and gold highlighter on her cheeks.

I actually am. Is that a problem?

It's okay this time. How's your hair?

Faith had never had a man ask her all these questions before a date. They usually just waited to see how she would look and give her a compliment then.

Send a picture. He texted.

Faith turned the vanity lights in her bathroom on and took a quick selfie. She waited for his response.

I'll see you in a minute.

Nerves overcame her as she attempted to wipe her eyeliner off. She could feel her hands shaking. This date was supposed to change her life and she feared she would ruin it by overusing her make-up skills. She wondered if he was used to a more "saved" looking woman who wore long dresses which is why he asked how short it was. Faith wanted to almost cry as she stepped into the living room to wait on his text that he was outside. If he didn't find her attractive, all bets were off.

Blake texted her five minutes later.

She peeked through the blinds and saw his red Tesla pull up to the curb. She watched people turn their heads to see who was driving.

Faith texted him her apartment number. Her heart began pounding as she heard his footsteps reach her door.

She opened the door before he could knock. A dozen roses were in his hand.

"Those are beautiful," Faith sighed. She put them down on the closest table to her.

"You look nice. You ready?"

Blake seemed a little colder than he did on the day they met. Being naturally competitive, this only made Faith want to impress him more.

"You look very handsome. Is that a new jacket?"

"It is. It's Burberry."

He had a sort of arrogance to him but it only made Faith want him more. His hazel eyes somewhat shimmered in the fading light of the afternoon. His curly hair carefully lay down on the side of his forehead. It was as if he had just taken a shower and let them hang instead of combing them backward.

Faith was still waiting for a compliment on her make-up and how she dressed but he led her down the stairs into his car without taking another look at her. Since his doors opened automatically, Faith sat in the car and crossed her legs.

She felt instantly turned on when he slipped into the driver's seat with his legs wide open. It was as if he was a pilot in the cockpit. Unlike most men where the car was a machine they were doing their best to operate, Blake took command of the fast, electric car and bent corners like he was a Formula 1 race car driver.

The conversation didn't start naturally so Faith thought she would make some small talk. "It's really nice weather today. It's not too hot or too cold. I didn't need to wear a big jacket."

"Yeah, well we're heading closer to the beach so it might be a little cooler."

He programmed his phone to play contemporary Gospel songs and turned the volume up. Faith was beginning to doubt that he liked her at all.

Once they reached the restaurant, the valet slipped into the driver's seat and Blake took her hand to lead her inside. They linked arms.

The hostess honored them immediately and led them to their table. A single candle was in the middle of it.

"You usually wear a lot of makeup?" Blake asked.

"I'm so sorry. Is it a problem?" Faith was naturally very sensitive so she could feel the tears begin to meet her eyes.

"No, it's no problem. You just have such a beautiful face. I would hate to see it covered with make-up all the time. I'm just used to dating women who are more natural."

Faith felt embarrassed and looked everywhere but in his eyes. She made a mental note that she would never wear make-up again in front of him. She would limit it to moisturizer and light mascara just so her eyes could pop.

She was already enamored with Blake who appeared intensely perfect. She even liked the way he read the menu. It was as if he had grown up in an etiquette school. They both ordered pasta. Blake took out his phone and claimed that he was checking his emails. Faith stared awkwardly in his direction and slowly grabbed the warm sourdough bread in the middle of the table, placing a piece in her mouth.

It was as if everything she did between then and when the date was over was being scrutinized. She sat with his back as straight as possible. Her legs were crossed at the ankle. She kept her elbows off the table and she made sure to always steer the conversation into a Christian topic.

"Do you do devotionals?" Blake asked looking over his menu.

Faith didn't do devotionals regularly but she

assumed that he wanted a woman who did. She was going to dust off her old devotional workbook that she had gotten for her birthday two years ago and complete it.

"Not really, I'm too busy with my preaching right now. I'm steady trying to open a church. I admire that you do. I love a woman that's serious about The Word."

"I'm very serious about God's word. I don't go a day without praying on a verse given to me."

Blake smiled. His eyes were illuminated by the candle in between them. Faith felt like she had scored one hundred points on the scoreboard and had to keep going to win.

Once the food came, Blake prayed by gently holding both of Faith's hands. His voice reverberated through her spine. His deep dimple pierced his cheek when he gave her a half smile.

Faith began to eat right away.

"You're not going to wait for the food to cool?" Blake asked with one eyebrow raised.

"Oh, I'm sorry. I was just so hungry."

He sat with her arms crossed and seemed to check the time on his phone. "So, let me know a little bit more about you."

Faith felt like she was on a job interview.

"What do you want to know?"
"Do you drink? Smoke?"

"Absolutely not."

"How often do you go to church?"

"Throughout the week."

"Why haven't you been snatched up already?" He said with a smirk.

"I was about to ask you the same thing. You told me you didn't have children?"

"No. I have none."

That still relieved Faith. She had been searching for a man that had no children for a long time. Her friend Tara had told her to forget it and that few men that were worth anyone's time were childless.

"I truly admire that. I never had children either and I always wanted to wait for marriage."

"What is your timeline when it comes to marriage?"

"I would like to be married in due time. I won't say in six months but not six years either."

Blake placed some of his Caesar salad onto his fork. "I like a woman who knows what she wants."

"Two years." Faith said softly.

Blake smiled. "One year for me."

Faith couldn't believe it. He had serious marriage plans and was also in the ministry.

"I plan on getting married either right before or right after I open my church."

"You plan on opening your church soon?"

"I plan on opening it very soon. I'm looking for a building as we speak that's why I was on my phone. I wasn't ignoring you. I have someone that's finding a building for me and I'm calculating all these overhead costs."

"Well, I'll be right there in the front row when it opens. I watched one of your videos the other night and you are a powerful speaker. I was blessed listening to you. I liked how you preached about David and Goliath. You put a different spin on it."

Blake moved his eyes back to his phone and then called the waiter over for the check.

Faith hoped she hadn't said anything wrong. She was already dreaming of their wedding and how elegant she would look in one of those big First Lady church hats. He made her heart flutter like a middle school girl crushing on a boy. She had just noticed how his long, thick eyelashes framed his eyes. The date would be over in less than an hour. It was time to lock him in.

After he paid with his credit card, the two stood up to leave the restaurant. Faith didn't want the night to be over. She wished it was more appropriate to sit on his lap and inhale more of his cologne. She wanted to move her mouth in between his neck and ear to kiss him.

As they entered his car, Faith mentally prayed to herself hoping that God would make him her husband.

She felt her phone vibrate and knew it was from Tara who wanted to know how the date went. Faith decided not to answer it until the date was completely over.

"I had a nice time. This was a lovely and blessed evening." Faith said softly.

"I thought it was beautiful as well. I had a wonderful time."

There was an awkward silence. Faith hoped he would ask her if they could go out again.

"It definitely was a lovely evening. I'm sure you had such a busy schedule being a pastor and all."

He looked at her out of the corner of his eye. "I did. God is good."

Faith felt herself becoming impatient.

"I don't usually go out but this was nice," she said crossing her leg across her thigh. "The dates I've been on, I've had to cut a few short. I didn't even meet many of them for a second date. It was a first date thing and then we stopped talking."

Blake's eyes were studying the road but she knew he was hanging onto her every word.

"You don't usually do second dates?"
"Oh no, I do. I just haven't found many men second-date worthy."

Blake chuckled. "So, I'm guessing you might find me second-date worthy?"

Faith looked out the window and tried to hide her smile. "Well, I definitely had a much better time with you.

It's not like I've been on hundreds of dates but this one certainly stands out. However, I'm probably competing with the other women you're courting."

"Me? Dating other women? No. I'm a one-woman man."

He pulled up to the curb next to her apartment and then walked her to her door. Their eyes locked in on each other and Blake took one more step forward. Faith could have sworn he wanted to kiss her.

"May I come in?" Blake asked.

Faith was shocked he would ask such a thing as a pastor. She never let a man inside her home before. It could lead to temptation. She didn't want to deny him but she didn't want to lose her virginity to anybody anytime soon. That man was especially not going to be someone who wasn't her husband.

"Well, I don't typically invite men in who I am not

in a relationship with nor married to. I had a wonderful time, but that invited temptation and I want to maintain my purity to God."

Blake raised one of his thick eyebrows. He slowly licked his lips. "Just the answer I was looking for. You truly are a woman of virtue. I'm also maintaining my virginity and I don't want to let it go anytime soon. God is preparing me for my wife."

Faith felt like jumping up and down. He was both saved and still a virgin. Her friend Tara swore only unattractive men were virgins. Faith couldn't wait to let her know how wrong she was.

"You have a wonderful evening, Faith. I'll call you tomorrow. Let's set something up either midweek or next weekend if you're free."

He pulled her in for a hug and Faith didn't want to let go.

"Yes, I'd love to."

"Maybe we can do some Bible study through *Facetime.* You're very well versed on God's word. I'd love to hear more."

"Wonderful, then it's settled. I'll text you before I go to bed. Let me know when you arrive home, Blake."

He nodded and blew her a kiss. She watched his body quickly pull down the stairs and swiftly enter his car. Faith kept her vision on him through her blinds. The rest of the night was like a dream. She was so caught up in her daydream of what life would be like with him, she couldn't remember how she removed her dress and slipped on her pajamas. Life was finally coming together in the exact way she had dreamed it would. Everyone had doubted her wait. God had been on her side the whole time.

Faith texted Blake forty-five minutes later to make sure that he arrived home safely.

I did, sweetheart. Thank you.

As soon as she received a text from him, she scrolled over to Faith's name to text her.

Girl, it was amazing!

Really? Call me?

Faith called her immediately. She was still trying to settle herself down.

"How was everything?"

"I have so much fun. He's such a gentleman. He really does carry himself like a pastor. He's very suave and I love the way he speaks. He didn't try to kiss me or anything."

"Well that's good. However, you've met some gentleman before. How is he different?"

"Well not only did he not want to kiss me, he is still holding out for a wife. I couldn't believe it. He's so handsome. You would think he would have been with several women by now but he hasn't."

"He's a virgin?"

"Yes! Can you believe that? It's so good. I knew there was something that was bringing us together. We were both waiting for 'the one.'"

Faith could tell Tara kept pausing to find the words to say. "Are you sure you're cool with that?"

"Why wouldn't I be? You don't find a man like that every day."

"Yeah, it's still odd."

Faith rolled her eyes. She couldn't believe her friend was so caught up in Blake's virginity as opposed to the type of man he was.

"I think it's a good thing. Actually, I think it's a wonderful thing. You don't find too many men that are willing to wait on their wife."

"I didn't say it wasn't a good thing, Faith. I just think it's a little strange."

"It's strange because he hasn't slept with hundreds of women? It's strange because he's so good looking?" Faith said with her voice beginning to crack. Tara had already met her happy ending so the least she could do was be happy for hers.

"Look, let's drop it. How was everything else?" Tara asked.

"It was a lovely restaurant. Of course, he paid. He drives a beautiful Tesla. I had actually never been in one of those before."

"You guys going out again?"

"We will. He actually told me that he wants to go out again either midweek or on the weekend next week. We might do something like a Bible Study. See, half these men I dated barely knew anything about God's word so it's very refreshing."

"Well, be careful. Be prayerful, friend," Tara said yawning.

"I will. Have a good night, Tara."

Faith ended the call and felt her eyes become heavy. She decided to turn her desk light on and read a Bible verse before she went to bed.

Once she put her phone on her charger, she noticed that she had missed a text from Blake.

She opened the message and saw he had left a Bible

verse.

Beware of false prophets who come to you in sheep's clothing but inwardly are ravening wolves. Matthew 7:15

Faith thought it was interesting but odd that he decided to send her that verse randomly.

I just wanted to give you something to read before bed. I reflect on this one a lot. I'm going to preach on this one on Sunday on my live video.

That's a good one. I was actually going to read something else but I like that one. I'll go on and flip over to Matthew. Faith texted back with a smile.

Faith read the verses before and after it. She thought it was a nice verse but it was a little strong to reflect on before bed. She flipped back to Psalms and started one of her favorite verses. She played some soft

Gospel music in the background and grabbed her highlighter and pen so she could write down a few of her reflections.

Did you read it? He texted three minutes later.

I did. I'm about to go to bed.

Good. I'll send you another in a few minutes. God's word is so important these days.

It truly is. I'm actually getting ready to go to bed right now so I'll talk to you later.

Faith put her Bible and devotional down on her nightstand.

No. Go to bed in an hour. I'll be up all night. Read the Bible right now. God told me to tell you that you need to dig deeper into his word.

Faith felt her heart palpitate and kept staring at his text. **Okay. I will. I'll do that, Pastor. ;)**

Good. He texted back. I'll be thinking about you, Sweetheart.

Turning her phone on silent, Faith drifted into a slumber with a smile on her face.

The next morning, Faith woke up to her alarm. It was a workday and she hadn't laid her clothes out for the next morning so she knew she was going to have to get out of the bed immediately.

Once she picked up her phone, she noticed that Blake had sent her at least fifteen texts asking her if she was up and asking her to read yet another Bible verse. He told her that he hoped she wasn't asleep and then finally said a short prayer for her.

She was about to put her phone down and then received a "Good Morning" text.

Good morning. Faith texted back.

I was thinking about you all night. I was just thinking about how hard it is to find a woman so invested in God's word.

I love how you are loving his word as well. I'm sorry I went to bed. I had work this morning and I was just so tired.

No worries. Text me when you get to work.

Faith showered and wore her hair in a sleek bun. Her work clothes consisted of a basic blue blouse, a black skirt, and black ballet flats.

What are you wearing? Blake texted.

Faith enjoyed how engaged he was with her. She

knew a lot of other women had to deal with the problem of ghosting but she knew Blake wasn't going anywhere anytime soon.

While she was getting dressed, she had been scrolling down his social media page to swoon at a few of his pictures. She saw that he had a tattoo of the Bible verse, "Be watchful, stand firm in the faith, act like men, be strong. Let all that you do be done in love. 1 Corinthians 16 13:14."

He didn't have a lot of pictures from when he was younger but she saw a few from when he first created his social media account.

Faith checked the mirror and then sent him a selfie.

Lookin real churchy. I like that about you.

Faith couldn't keep herself from grinning until she got to her car. She promised to text him once she got to work.

While in the car, Faith called her mother from the Bluetooth setup in her car.

"Hello?"

"Hello, Mother. How are you doing?"

"I'm well. You on your way to work?"

"Yeah. I am."

"What happened? You sound like you wanna say something," her mother laughed.

"I finally met the man I think is going to be my husband."

"Where'd you meet him?"

"At the new pastor's conference. The one that was at the hotel."

"Faith, you're not a new pastor. What were you doing there?"

"His name is Blake McPherson. He's an up and coming minister. He has his own online ministry and is about to open a church. He's never been married and has no children."

"Now, does he meet all the physical qualities you want? I know how you can get."

"He's light skinned, has beautiful hair, six feet tall, and such a gentleman, Mother. You're definitely going to get a chance to meet him."

"Well, I hope so. Don't get too excited. Is he calling you?"

"Every night. He texts sometimes but he's always keeping up with me."

"Well, I'll be praying for you. He sounds like a nice young man."

Faith arrived at her school's parking lot and lugged her purse and briefcase out of the car.

Did you arrive at work yet? Blake texted.

Faith couldn't believe how he was able to pinpoint the exact time she arrived at work.

I am. It's nice to hear from you.

Faith was somewhat confused that he had seemed distant during most of their last date but was suddenly almost obsessed with her. She couldn't be too mad because she was quite obsessed with him too. She had tried to find mutual friends that they had in common through social media so she could ask them more about him. However, every time she tried, nothing turned up.

He sent her a Bible verse to reflect on and she sent one back. He was like the best friend she never had. Faith could talk to him about anything. His texts helped to give her the extra boost of energy she needed to get through her day.

He told her that he would be busy for most of the day but wanted to check in from time to time. They had set up another day to meet for dinner next week which made Faith begin to look online for another dress that Blake would find suitable. He was all about modesty so she wanted to make sure that she stuck to a certain cut and length while searching for another dress.

"Got another date?" Martha whispered looking over Faith's shoulder.

"With the same man. He asked if we could meet for dinner again next week. He wants me to bring my Bible and everything so we can study together. I'm just looking for a specific dress."

"Like what?"

"Something more modest."

"Why?"

"He prefers that I dress more conservatively. I think he's just used to that. He's a pastor so, essentially, I have to look like a pastor's wife."

Martha raised an eyebrow. "But, you're not married to him and he's already controlling what you wear? You don't even know him that well."

"I enjoy dressing modestly. I was actually going to start taking up some new dressing habits before I met him."

"Just don't change yourself for any man, Faith. The right one isn't going to change you. Besides, how open is he about himself trying to have control suddenly?"

Faith purchased the dress in her digital shopping cart.

"You got to make sacrifices sometimes when God sends you 'the one.' I'm not doing anything bad. Haven't you ever heard of the saying 'dress for the job you want and not the job you have?'"

Martha slowly nodded, pulling her hand from Faith's shoulder, then calmly stepping away from her coworker's desk. "Just be prayerful, hun. That's all I'm saying."

Chapter 3

Bible study sessions were becoming more frequent. Blake told her things that she would have never been able to decipher herself. He spoke from God's word as a preacher and not just someone who had a simple interest in studying the Bible. Their phone calls could last into the wee hours of the morning on weekends. Any problem she had at work, he always had a Bible verse or words of encouragement. Suddenly, she began to lean on him more than Tara and her mother.

Blake was all she thought about and since his birthday was coming up, she wanted to make it as special as possible. Following work on a Wednesday afternoon, Faith asked Blake what size shirts he wore and his waist measurements. She wanted to purchase a suit so he could wear it on his live preaching videos on social media.

He sent her his measurements quickly via text. She spent two hundred dollars on a dark blue suit at the local mall. It was on sale, but used to be nine hundred dollars before it made its way to the clearance rack.

Faith invited him out to dinner at a seafood restaurant in Manhattan Beach. It was expensive but she wanted to give him the best she could. Because he was having a church event that afternoon, they would meet each other.

Faith arrived there first with the suit in her hand wrapped in a garment bag. Blake came in thirty minutes later than she expected but she stood to greet him as soon as their eyes met. Blake appeared exhausted but he still hugged her.

"What is this?" He said looking at the garment bag. "A suit? Sweetheart, you didn't have to do that."

"No, but I wanted to," Faith said, unzipping it. "I

wanted you to have something else nice for your live events."

"Well, I should have known when you asked me. I actually don't like to get suits off the rack because I really have to tailor them."

Faith raised an eyebrow. She was sure that all suits had to be tailored.

"I have unusually narrow shoulders for a guy so I just like to buy my own clothes. It's okay though. You didn't know."

Faith felt her stomach drop and tears began to form in the corners of her eyes. She felt a wave of embarrassment run through her body. Blake sat down and grabbed the menu. "I'm not really a seafood guy but I hope they have some salad. Maybe I can have bread."

"I was sure you said you go to seafood places every

once in a while."

"Yeah. I just wasn't in the mood today. It's okay, love. It's my birthday. We're here to have a good time. Don't sweat it."

"Well, I'm sorry I ruined your birthday." Faith kept her eyes focused on her menu hoping that pretending to read it would calm her down and keep the tears out of her eyes.

"You didn't ruin my birthday, Love." Blake reached out his hand and touched hers. He gently rubbed it and then wiped the corner of her eyes where a tear was forming. "I'm a little picky. I've always been that way. It's not your fault. I just like things a certain way."

Faith had done everything for the date to make sure that he was pleased. Her dress fell to her calves and her breasts were covered leaving out her neckline and a turquoise necklace.

"You look beautiful, Sweetheart. You know what else you are?"

"What?" Faith said wiping a tear.

"My woman. I think we need to make it official. How'd you like that?"

Faith couldn't believe what she just heard. The words she had been waiting to hear had finally happened. She had won. This beautiful specimen of a man was one step close to becoming her husband.

"I'd love that very much. I really would."

Blake lifted her hand and kissed it. The waitress came by their table and asked what they would like to drink. They were so locked into each other's eyes, they ignored the young woman who decided to come back and ask them later.

"What made you ask today?" Faith asked.

"Why would I wait? I felt like you've been mine since we first met. I was going to ask sooner or later."

Faith straightened her posture and was beaming for the rest of the night. She excused herself to the bathroom and texted Tara that she and Blake had just become an official couple. She didn't wait for her response and walked back to the table with a burst of energy.

"You excited for the next step?"

"Being with you? This is a wonderful step." Faith said, grabbing his hands. She locked her fingers with his.

"I mean the next one. When I make you my wife."

"Well, that won't be for a long time from now."

"It does? I plan on opening my church in six months. I want to open it with a first lady. I'm not going into my new building single. I believe God is leading me into the right path with the right woman and I want to move along in His word."

Faith was stunned. It was a partial proposal but it was good enough for her.

"So, who's going to say it first?" Blake said.

"Say what? I love you?"

"See, I knew it would be you. That's something we can tell our grandkids one day."

Faith felt like she was floating on a cloud for the rest of the night. Not even their first kiss woke her up from her slumber.

Her prayers were being laid out before her much quicker than she expected. Blake was "the one." From that point on, her life was finally going to unfold.

Two months later, in the midst of their whirlwind romance, Blake finally found a building in West Los Angeles. It was close to Hollywood which Blake wanted. He was trying to start a church that encouraged more young people to join.

Before the church was open, Blake had acquired thousands of weekly viewers on his live social media ministry. Faith had begun to work on his social media as well and had become one of his promoters and used the account to engage with the audience.

In the middle of summer, Vision Church was open. It was a spacious building that included a balcony and two projector screens where the altar was. Faith and Blake had invested a lot of their own money as well as donations to purchase seats, a crystal podium, a cameraman, and a media crew.

Their first Sunday was supposed to be in two weeks. From their social media invite, two hundred people promised to go.

Faith's excitement was bubbling over. She had purchased several new outfits and planned on wearing her hair long, with a weave for fullness just the way Blake liked it.

However, there was one thing still hanging over her as opening day got closer.

"Blake," Faith said while they sipped tea at one of their business meetings at a West Hollywood coffee shop. "I'm so excited for you. I'm excited for us. It's just that I thought things would be a little different by the time we got here."

"What do you mean? Is there something wrong?" Blake said carefully scrolling through the emails on his phone.

"I mean that I thought we would be a married couple by now. I won't be starting as Vision Church's first lady. I'll be the first girlfriend."

Faith's voice lowered and she watched Blake put his phone down and sigh.

"I'm sorry, Baby. I had just been so busy. I do want to be an official married couple."

"How will we do that by the time your church opens? I guess you want to wait until after."

"I actually don't. I want a destination wedding and all I need to do is set it up and we're good."

"You mean we could get married in Jamaica by like tomorrow?"

"Your choice. Purchase your dress. I'll get my tux and we'll go."

"What about our parents? I still haven't even met your mother."

"She's still sickly. I wouldn't want to put all that stress on her."

"What about *my* mother?" Faith asked.

"You can bring her. Bring Tara and her husband too. I'll bring my assistant pastor and best friend since childhood, Byron."

Faith had just been seeing Byron lately. He had been in charge of gathering new members and interviewing people for leadership roles. They didn't act as close as Blake claimed.

"Then we'll do it. Let's get married." Blake said sweetly.

"Aren't you supposed to do something first?"

"You want to be surprised or you want me to get you that seven-carat diamond at Cartier right now?"

Faith nodded her head and couldn't keep the tears from flowing out of her eyes.

Blake lifted his tea cup which prompted her to lift hers. "To my wife."

"To my husband," Faith answered.

They reached over and kissed. Part of Blake's tongue slipped past her lips. She felt sweat drip down her armpits. While her eyes were closed, he wiped a tear from her eye and kissed her on the forehead.

"I love you, First Lady."

"I love you too, Pastor."

❖

Their destination wedding in Jamaica was more beautiful than Faith could have pictured. She wore a simple white gown similar to what Meghan Markle wore at her wedding. Blake was dressed in a cream suit with tails. His hazel eyes reflected the clear blue water the entire time they were there.

Only Byron, Tara, Tara's husband David, and Faith's mother were in attendance. Byron led the ceremony and Tara used her Nikon to take pictures. Faith's mother was crying the entire time.

Directly following the ceremony, Faith was grabbed by Tara who hugged her for what seemed like an eternity.

"I'm so proud of you friend. You really did it. You waited, and look what God found for you. You inspire me."

"Thank you, Tara. I'm really happy. I couldn't

have found a better man."

Faith floated toward her new husband following the reception dinner and sat on his lap. She allowed him to kiss her on the cheek and whisper how much he loved her in her ear. Everyone looked over in their direction in awe. The two of them looked perfect together.

That evening, Faith couldn't take her mind off what was going to happen next. She was finally going to lose her virginity. She wondered if it would hurt or if he would be gentle. He was a gentle kisser so maybe he would ease into her and not force himself inside like she had heard what happened to her friends as teenagers.

In their beachside hotel room, Faith put on a white silk pajama set that exposed most of her breasts and her long legs. She lied down on the pillows waiting for him. He was brushing his teeth in the bathroom.

Minutes later, Blake walked in and immediately moved his eyes away from her. He put on a T-shirt and turned to his side to go to bed.

"Blake," she whispered. "Don't we have some business to take care of."

Faith kissed his ear and then rubbed his shoulder.
"I'm too tired tonight."
"You mean we can't do anything?" Faith nervously chuckled.

"You're that obsessed with losing your virginity? I mean we *just* got married."

Faith reached over for his penis and he took his elbow from under the covers and pushed her back.

"I'm not in the mood right now, Faith. Marriage isn't all about sex. We need to consecrate this marriage with prayer first before we move into the physical."

Faith had never heard of a marriage being

consecrated before sex but he was the Bible scholar and she wasn't.

Part of her wondered if he was truly attracted to her or had a small penis and was embarrassed.

"Blake, I don't care what it looks like. I just want you."

"Faith! Say your prayers and go to sleep! It was a long day!"

Stunned by his tone, she got out of the bed, said her prayers, and kept her eyes open thinking about him for the next hour. Finally, her eyes became too heavy for her to hold onto her anxiety anymore.

Maybe he was right? Sex was not the key ingredient to marriage. Neither of them had had sex before so it probably made him nervous.

"I'm sorry, Honey. I'll wait until we're both totally ready."

"Thank you, Baby," Blake whispered and kissed her once more on the forehead.

Faith said one more silent prayer to herself and prayed for her new husband. When they finally committed to sex, she knew it would be the best experience either of them had ever witnessed.

Within a month, Vision Church was officially open. The new worship center opened with almost two hundred people in attendance. Many of the parishioners were actors, models, and singers in Hollywood that were continuing to advance their career. Faith and Blake knew that their church had the chance to be the new "it" church of Black Hollywood.

It had been only three weeks and Faith and Blake had also begun to dominate social media. They had taken new professional pictures and revamped Vision Church's social media page to include both of them.

Faith wanted to find her place in the women's ministry. She had always been complimented on her speaking voice and great attention to detail.

Blake encouraged her to quit her job as an office assistant for the school district and pursue the ministry full-time with him.

She was unsure and, once she told Tara and her mother, they created doubts in her mind. Tara knew Faith loved children and being financially independent, which she had gone to school for.

"You sure you gonna quit all your benefits and your pension?" Tara said over the phone one Saturday afternoon.

"I really think being in the ministry with my husband is my calling. I don't see myself doing anything else."

"If you say so," Tara sighed.

While Faith was on the phone, Blake had his head on her lap. He had been ill all day.

After Faith ended the call, she rubbed his head. "You should really get those stomach ulcers checked out, Baby."

"I'm good. I got some medicine in there. I'll take it. Was that your friend telling you about not being in ministry full time?"

"Yes," Faith said slowly. Faith knew Blake had always had an issue with her best friend. Tara was raised Catholic so Blake was convinced she was headed straight to hell.

"You shouldn't talk to her anymore. She sounds like a devil. Only Satan wants to pull you away from God's Word. You know that's a fact," Blake groaned. He tossed his head to the other side.

Faith rubbed her fingers through his hair and then eased her fingers down his back. "Okay, Sweetheart. I'm not going anywhere."

Faith blocked Tara's number and continued to nurse her husband to health with everything in her power including prayer.

Within six months, Vision Church was one of the fastest growing African American churches in Southern California. Most of their membership ranged between the ages of twenty-five years old and thirty-five years old. Many of them were willing to take on new leadership roles within the church. Faith felt like she had a new family at Vision Church. Everyone was supportive and the single women in the church now looked up to her as a beacon of hope.

She was encouraged to write a book about Christian marriage by a few of the ladies involved in the women's ministry. After finding a publisher, her book became a bestseller online and in stores. Within a month, it was one of the fastest selling self-help books. Her husband had also tried his hand at writing and published a devotional for men under forty. Their social media presence was steadily growing.

Money was coming in quickly. Because of donations to their church, offerings, and the money made from Vision Church's merchandise, they were already making six figures between them. They were on schedule to make their first million by the end of the year. T-shirts and personalized Bibles with Vision Church's logo were selling by the hundreds weekly. Their live service was still popular across the nation. It seemed like their social media viewers were becoming fans of just Faith and Blake and not just there to listen to them speak.

Faith could tell hundreds of young ladies on social media and in church had a crush on Blake. She heard them call him "Drake" and "El Debarge" which she had compared him to when they first met. Faith was beginning to feel more pressure to look her best every Sunday and even when she ventured to the grocery store to make sure that she represented her popular husband well. Blake demanded that her hair and nails were always done. He didn't want her to wear anything revealing but he preferred that everything she put on was designer. Faith now owned dozens of Chanel and Versace dresses just to wear to church. She had never been much of a "label whore" but Blake refused to be seen in anything less than what could be found on Rodeo Drive. He purchased everything she put on so she kept her mouth closed.

Their sex life hadn't improved much and Faith was beginning to feel twinges in her ovaries to have children someday. He pleased her in every way but inserting his penis inside her. Sex was beginning to become something that Faith daydreamed about but was afraid to ask about for fear that Blake would blow up on her. According to him, it was her job to keep him happy and to pray for him.

"I married a praying wife, right?" Blake would say whenever she questioned something he did that she didn't agree with. A few times, he had even physically pushed her.

The couple now lived in a luxury condo during the week in Downtown L.A. They owned a sprawling mansion in Calabasas but it was usually too far to travel to since most of their business was conducted in Los Angeles.

Faith was beginning to enjoy her new life of luxury. Online, it seemed like she was living like a queen but secretly she longed to start a family. It hurt her every time she looked online or saw women carrying their little bundles of joy on the streets.

There was a New Mothers Ministry at their church which triggered her so she stayed as far away as she could from them.

That evening, on one those unusual nights when both Blake and Faith were at home, Faith couldn't hold it in any longer.

"Baby, I really think I'm ready for kids."

Blake didn't look up from his cellphone and pretended he didn't hear her for a few moments.

"Kids? Now? Why do we want to make our lives so much more complicated? We haven't even reached the peak of our careers yet."

Faith sighed. "Well when is it ever going to be the right time? I'm tired of waiting. I'm forty years old. Who knows how many eggs I have left?"

"Probably plenty and you're worrying too much about it. Just let things happen."

Blake stretched his legs out on the plush couch and put his hands behind his head. His cellphone rested on his chest.

"Until when? Until I get menopausal? You are so selfish."

"You're the one selfish who wants to have a baby as busy as we are!"

"You promised we would start a family!"

"Not right away!"

"It's been five months and we have yet to consummate our marriage."

"I won't have sex with a woman who keeps falling into sin such as jealousy of what other women have. You only want a baby because you see other women have one!"

Faith began sobbing so hard, her chest began to hurt. She fell to the floor on her knees and began to hyperventilate.

"You're going overboard, Faith. It's not that serious!"

"I want a baby! You act like we have no money and can't support one! Why are you doing this to me?"

Blake left the room and went upstairs to his office slamming the door behind him.

They didn't speak to one another for the rest of the evening.

❖

Although Faith felt as popular as Beyoncé as their ministry was growing, it still bothered her that her contact with other people was limited to her husband. Blake traveled a lot so she was left home alone most of the time.

Her entertainment had become reading the Bible, preparing her Bible Study notes since she led it every Wednesday night, and social media. Ever since she had cut Tara off, she had tried to make more connections with other women at church, but they were either too starstruck or jealous of her. She had become a master at spotting the women who were looking at her husband a little too hard. She knew quite a few women at Vision Church felt that she wasn't pretty enough to be with him. She had heard the rumors and they hurt, but she loved Blake and knew he loved her.

Blake appeared to be more jealous of the potential men she was talking to. Every time she commented under another preacher's post online, he would text her to ask how she knew him. Faith never did but once they got into an argument because he thought she was lying.

Tara had crossed her mind one evening. She

wondered what her friend was up to and if she was still thinking about her. She had been so busy that she hadn't been able to visit her social media page in a long time.

Once she went on her page, tears formed in her eyes. Tara had begun to hang out more with her other friends. They had recently gone on a girl's trip to Cuba, and Tara was expecting once again. Faith unblocked Tara's number and texted her.

Hey Tara! How's everything?

Faith decided to start on reading some emails while she waited for her reply.

Tara had left her read receipts on and it said that she had just read the message.

Faith assumed Tara was busy and would reply to her later. A few hours passed and Faith still didn't hear anything. Panic was beginning to set it that her friend was truly done with her. She wanted to text her to ask for forgiveness but didn't know how she should start that conversation.

She and Tara had known each other since they were children. She used to tell her everything and, because of Faith's actions, their relationship was irreparable.

She hadn't spoken as much to her mother lately who had visited her church only once. Her mother thought that the crowd was too young for her. Vision Church was almost cult-like. If you weren't supporting the church, then you were against it.

However, maintaining a membership of that size required a lot of work, and Faith had little time left over to keep up with her close relationships. Even her relationship with Blake seemed like a business partnership only, at times.

❖

On a rare Sunday evening when Faith and Blake were home at the same time, their Downtown condo was buzzing. Vision Church's leadership including the Minister of Music, Minister of Hospitality, the Assistant Pastor, and the Minister of the Spanish Ministry.

Faith made fried chicken, macaroni and cheese, collard greens, and cornbread. She had never been into cooking but Blake demanded that she learn. According to him, it was a first lady's duty to prepare a meal for her husband.

She labored over the meal with grease and sweat combined on her forehead. Blake chatted in the other room with the men with obnoxious laughter trailing behind every other sentence.

Faith had been so nervous about cooking the best meal she could; she hadn't been able to get any other work done. She was supposed to have a meeting with her publicist about appearing on a daytime talk show. None of her emails had been answered that day, which was starting to make her anxious.

First, the fried chicken was done and then the scent of the collard greens wafted into the living room.

"You ready, Baby?" Blake called out loudly.

"You all can start making your way into the kitchen."

All at once, the men grabbed a plate. Blake demanded that she use their best dishes and not paper plates. That was going to be more work for Faith but she calmly accepted it and refused to say anything.

Faith ate by herself in the kitchen while the men took their dinners into the living room to continue to chat with the TV on.

A few minutes later, she went to the guest bathroom and it was occupied. She ran upstairs to her bathroom that was occupied as well. Her last resort was to use Blake's private bathroom that was connected to his office.

She heard footsteps behind her but didn't give them a second thought. Her hand was about to twist the knob to open it but a hand gripped hers with so much force, she was startled.

"What are you doing?" Blake snapped.

"Both bathrooms were occupied. I had to go so I decided to use this one."

Faith was still breathing heavily.

"We have our own bathrooms. You were just going in there to sneak around."

"Blake this is *our* house. It isn't just *your* house. Why are you doing this?"

"You need to learn how to take directions. I have asked

you to do something and you're being insubordinate."

"I am not a child, Blake. I'm a grown woman. I don't need you to tell me what I should be doing."

Blake forcefully pushed her against the door and looked around. Minister Sutton was coming upstairs to find the bathroom. Faith felt his grip leave her throat.

"We only have two bathrooms. Check the one downstairs. It's next to the pool table."

Faith watched him give Blake a thumbs-up and proceeded to go downstairs.

Faith escaped from upstairs and went back into the kitchen. Blake slowly followed behind her. The two didn't speak to each other again until the guests left. Faith used that time to check her emails and keep up her correspondence with her publicist. Every once in a while, Faith would check her social media and let her heart melt looking at all the happy families with children on her feed.

Someone else she knew from work had just had a baby girl. She had gotten pregnant at forty-one which instantly inspired Faith. Possibly, her time wasn't up yet.

It was nine o'clock in the evening and the guests had left a couple hours ago. Blake had locked himself in his office to work. Faith had turned on some soft Gospel music and placed a pillow underneath her head to relax. She poured a glass of apple cider and closed her eyes.

She heard Blake come down the stairs and she could feel him standing over her.

"Yes?" Faith asked. Her heart began beating rapidly.

He sat next to her on the couch. His back extended on the back of the couch and his hands remained on his lap. Faith watched his leg tremble. She immediately sat up and began rubbing his back.

"What's wrong, Dear?"

He took a deep sigh. "I've been thinking a lot about what you said."

"About what? What did I say?"

"I know you want children."

"I do."

Faith grabbed his hands and looked into his eyes. "What did you want to say, Baby?"

"I think it's best that we adopt. I don't think we should bring more children into this world if there are so many that need to be adopted."

Faith slowly shook her head. "You know adoption costs money, Baby."

"But you're forty. You'll be forty-one in a few weeks. How could you possibly have a child?"

"I could possibly have a child because, with God, all things are possible. I just saw one of my old friends have a baby at forty-one. It's not impossible at all."

"She probably had to get science involved and I don't believe in playing with God."

Faith stood crossing her arms. "Well we're not even interacting with God in the first place because we haven't even had sex to even create one. You're always blaming me."

"You don't like everything else we do? I don't please you?"

"Blake, I also married to have a sexual relationship and not just a praying one."

"So, you just don't appreciate me at all?"

"Why do you avoid me? What's your problem? What

are you hiding?"

"I told you that I'm waiting until the right moment. Our marriage has to be consecrated beforehand. You're just trying to bring the devil into our marriage!"

"No, I'm trying to have a child and you're suggesting we adopt some random child."

Blake violently shook his head. "I can't believe I married someone as cold as you are. I guess you think less of a child because they're in foster care or in the system. Just evil."

"This conversation is over, Blake." Faith's voice began to crack. She locked herself into her office and shut herself away from the world for the rest of the evening.

Blake was leaving on a business trip in the morning and she didn't care how long it would be until she saw him again.

Something wasn't right. He was hiding something but, although he was her husband, he was an anointed man. Her fear wouldn't allow her to believe that she wouldn't be walking on thin ice with God if she investigated any further.

Chapter 4

"So, where's my grandbaby?" Faith's mother chuckled on the phone on a rainy Thursday afternoon.

Faith sighed but knew her mother meant well. All mothers wanted grandchildren but her situation was out of the ordinary. Ever since, she and Blake had been arguing about intimacy, she decided to avoid the conversation altogether. He was usually traveling or busy so it had been easy to avoid interacting with him at all.

"Mother, you know I don't know the answer to that question. I'm forty years old. I'm almost forty-one. I might be out of the running by now."

"What are you talking about? Your aunt, my sister, had Byron at forty-one. It's not too late. You still getting your period?"

"Mother, a lot of women my age are having to use science or test tubes to have kids."

"I rebuke that. You and Blake can have one naturally."

She heard the grease from the pan her mother was cooking in pop. Faint daydreams of her cooking for small children at a stove popped into her head. She missed the days when she would smell her mother's cooking from her room and anxiously await to come into the kitchen and taste it.

"Well, Blake and I haven't been able to see each other for a few days. He's so busy. The church has been growing lately and I think he can barely keep up with all the new responsibilities."

"That's no excuse. I mean, do you want children?

If you don't want them, that's between you and Blake."

"No, Mother. I want them. I do. I want at least two. Blake grew up an only child. He doesn't have a big connection to his family anyway. I want to be able to give him that."

Blake texted her fifteen minutes ago but Faith hadn't felt her phone vibrate since she had been on the phone with her mother. He texted her numerous times to see what she was doing. Each text became more aggressive than the last.

Why aren't you texting me back? Who are you with? What are you doing? Blake texted back to back.

"Mother, let me call you back. This is Blake on the other line."

Faith called Blake immediately.

"Honey, what's going on?" Faith's hands were

shaking so much she thought she was going to drop the phone.

"Who's that in the background?" Blake fumed.

Faith turned the volume down on the TV; clips of Malcolm X were playing on a documentary she was watching.

"Who? Malcom X?"

"It just sounded like someone was in the background."

"No one is over here. I'm just looking for you to come home. Are you on your way?"

"Yeah. I got to take care of a few things and then I'll be home tonight. I'm sorry, Baby. I just love you so much and I'm just afraid of losing you."

"You don't have to worry about that, Baby. I'm here."

Faith ended the call and waited for his arrival. He demanded home cooked food whenever he was home so she decided to whip something up as quickly as she could before he arrived.

There was pasta in the cupboard and some green vegetables that she could steam so she began to zip around her kitchen until she was sweating. Blake walked in an hour later.

He didn't greet her and lied on the couch with his phone in one hand.

Faith left the kitchen to kiss him on the forehead.

"My new youth pastor, Cameron, is going to be here soon. You'll have enough food right?"

He had one eyebrow raised.

"Of course, Sweetheart."

"We'll be in my office to discuss a few things. I don't want a whole lot of interruptions."

"Don't worry. I'll be out of your way. It's just I'd like to get some time with you at some point this evening."

She watched him nod his head but his eyes drifted back to his phone.

Faith could feel distance growing between them each day. It didn't matter how many meals she cooked or how hard she prayed, Blake was always upset about something. She knew that running Vision Church was a difficult full time job. The membership was growing but, since it was a church that was geared toward young people, he didn't receive the hefty tithes of churches with an again membership roll. He was either complaining about money or some of his "lazy" assistants he wanted to fire. Faith wanted to soothe him but he was always finding a way to distance himself from her.

They had yet to be intimate but oral sex had blown her mind. Blake knew how to use his tongue in ways she never imagined. She would scream until he forced a pillow in her mouth. He massaged her, rubbed oils on her, and knew how to use ice cubes to harden and then lick her nipples. He was freaky but every time she reached down to his crotch, he would move it away and say he wasn't ready. Once, he had asked if she had been tested because he didn't want to pass anything to each other.

It was a frustrating experience but Blake had given her a life of luxury. Based on her social media profile, she knew her old coworkers had to be insanely jealous.

With trips to Dubai and shopping sprees in Milan, Faith was deciding to hold on. Eventually, a child would appear in her arms. Patience was a virtue.

An hour later, Cameron knocked on their door. Faith knew Blake had wanted to eat something heartier than pasta but she was sure they were both tired of fighting.

Faith watched Blake greet Cameron by shaking his hand. The two men sat on the couch and then proceeded to discuss business. Faith walked toward Cameron and shook his hand. She then sat down and joined in the conversation. Cameron was a much younger man that reminded her of one of her nephews. He was energetic and brought a lively energy into their home.

"Where are you originally from, Cameron?"

"Chicago."

"My mother's from there. I used to go all the time," Faith added.

"Really? So, are you a Bears or Cubs fan?"

"Both! I've never been into California teams."

"I didn't know you liked sports, Faith," Blake said softly.

"I do, we just never got the chance to talk about it. You know everything with you is Bible first, and then everything else."

"Well, we should all go to a Bears or Cubs game when they come to Los Angeles," Cameron began. "Thanks to God, I know a fellow fan now. It's hard to find diehard fans in the L.A. area."

Cameron reminded her of a younger Morris Chestnut. He had flawless dark skin, an athletic build, and bright teeth that he showed completely when he laughed. He had a long, thick beard cut carefully around his chin and his athletic outfit was comfortable but still appeared as if he put some thought into it. He was handsome but Faith thought of him as a younger brother or someone she could mentor.

Faith found out she had more in common with Cameron and the two began to dominate the conversation. They enjoyed the same restaurants in L.A., was raised in the Pentecostal church, and attended inner city schools.

Faith could tell that Blake was unusually quiet but eventually interrupted them and said that they should start eating.

"Yes! Let me go and make those plates quickly. I'm sorry, it's pasta today. I didn't have time for something more soul food."

"Are you kidding?" Cameron laughed. "I love pasta. I'm from Chicago and it's a lot of Italians out there so you eat it almost every time you go out for dinner."

Faith caught Blake's eyes which began to narrow. His lips pursed into a thin line. Faith couldn't imagine what was wrong with him. Blake had always stressed making good connections with the ministry team at Vision Church. Now that she was doing so, he was clearly upset. There was nothing about Cameron she wanted. He was only twenty-four. He'd be a nice catch for one of her young nieces but not for her.

"Dinner is served!" Faith called from the kitchen.

Cameron walked in quickly with Blake slowly following behind him. Blake attempted to dominate the conversation again with church business and scripture. However, the conversation eventually drifted back into Faith and Cameron's more lighthearted conversation.

"Pastor McPherson, let's just enjoy ourselves for now. We can talk business anytime. God is good!"

Faith swore steam was shooting out of Blake's ears. He used his phone for the remainder of the dinner. Luckily, Faith was able to swing the conversation back to the last Cubs game she saw and pull the tension out of the air.

After dinner, Faith cleaned the table and walked Blake and Cameron to the door. Both men decided to end their chat on the way to Cameron's car downstairs.

Blake returned ten minutes later.

She knew he was in the kitchen while she was loading the dishwasher but a dish slipped out of her hand once she felt his grip on her neck.

Faith couldn't move. The shards of the glass covered her bare feet.

"So, it looks like you and Cameron have a lot in common. Why don't you go follow him home?"

Faith stepped over the broken porcelain and quickly put on her slippers. "What are you talking about?"

128

"I didn't know you liked young men. You and him were just having the time of your lives."

"Blake," Faith said, crossing her arms. "You can't be serious. You know I love you. Cameron reminds me of my nephew. He's like a child. He just happens to have roots from Chicago like I do."

"I saw you looking him up and down like a common whore. Had I known I was marrying a Jezebel, I would have never walked down that aisle."

The tears in Faith's eyes wouldn't stop flowing. She felt nauseous and gripped the back of one of the kitchen stools to keep her balance. "Blake, I had no intentions for him. I was just being friendly."

"Being friendly and looking at the front of his sweatpants? You weren't slick, woman!"

Faith tried to remember what he was talking about.

He never noticed a penis print on Cameron's sweats. She never looked at that on a man.

"Blake, that is not what you saw."

Blake took a glass and threw it against the wall causing their pampered Chihuahua, Chanel, to start barking. Faith closed her eyes and covered her head.

"I know what I saw, woman!"

"Blake, I am not going to sit here and lie to you. I believe that I will never reach those heavenly gates if I don't commit myself to the truth and nothing but the truth. I did not have any lust in my heart for that man."

Faith felt like she was trying to prove her case to a grand jury. Blake's right eye began to twitch and then he broke down in tears. He kneeled and sobbed at Faith's feet.

"I just don't want to lose you! I know you think I'm

less of a man."

"No, Sweetheart. Of course not." Faith bent down to his level and stroked his hair backward. "Blake, I love you. I'm not going anywhere. Why don't you believe me?"

"Because, I had trouble feeling enough love from my family growing up. That's why I removed myself from them. You're all I have, Faith. You're all I have."

"And that's why I want a family with you, my love." Faith whispered in his ear.

They were both dangerously inches away from sharp glass. She helped him stand back up and then they both sat on the couch. She sat on his lap and wrapped her arms around his neck.

"I'm your family, Baby. I'll never leave you."

She let him sob into her chest until he fell asleep.

Times like this was when she wished she knew more about his family background but he had been secretive about his past since the day they met. He felt that if God brought him through it, it was useless to make constant mention of the unfortunate details from his past.

❖

The church had grown considerably in a little less than a year. Although Faith had expected the amount of families to increase, there were more single men and women. Most of their membership included millennials between the ages of twenty-five and thirty-five. Faith felt old because she couldn't identify with many of the young ladies in the church that were only a couple years out of college and were years away from settling down with a husband and children.

Vision Church had relocated closer to the Hollywood Hills. Thinking that their membership would decline, they had gained hundreds of actors, producers, singers, and musicians. Many of them were new Christians and had never attended church in their life. Vision Church was becoming one of the trendiest places to be on Sunday morning.

Their morning service carried on like a concert with electric guitars, drums, and professional singers. Trap Gospel was featured every other Sunday afternoon after Blake preached. Everyone could give their offering over an app and all members were encouraged to pin their location if they took pictures. The church even had its own geofilter and several hashtags they could apply to videos of the service. Blake made sure the service was live-streamed so people around the world could tune in.

However, what bothered Faith the most was that the church was leaning further away from the traditional Pentecostal views she held dear. Blake had promised her that "God's word" would remain the same but he was beginning to stray further away from it.

Faith noticed that Blake never mentioned

homosexuality for fear that many of his openly gay members would revolt and leave. To her shock, he encouraged it. Faith felt that God loved everyone, including those who were homosexual, but she also thought that the Bible should be followed in its entirety.

Not only did Blake overlook homosexuality but he also didn't speak against adultery, prostitution, drugs, gambling, and greed. The church was becoming more of a "spiritual center" as opposed to a church and Faith was beginning to feel lost. Blake didn't make sure his membership got "saved" and spoke in tongues. Rarely were his sermons about sin.

Faith and Blake argued later that evening because someone had sent a complaint online about Faith's women's Sunday school. Apparently, she had used too many stereotypes about what it meant to be a woman and a masculine lesbian woman was offended.

"What are you talking about?" Faith said while

they were on their way to the Stellar Awards. Blake was in a black tuxedo while Faith wore a long, emerald green dress with one shoulder out. She noticed that Blake no longer talked about what she wore if it revealed skin. She could tell that he wanted them to seem as young as possible. The membership was getting younger so they would have to keep up.

"DJ was offended when you said that a real woman puts her makeup on in the morning and takes care of business. You kept talking about what a real woman looks like."

"How is that a problem? I had a lot of people agreeing with me. It was literally one person that walked out. I didn't realize what I said was offensive to everyone."

Faith gripped the side of her seat and felt her stomach spin around.

"Look, I'm not telling you what to do but I just want us to start choosing our words carefully."

She spotted his new white gold Rolex peek from underneath the sleeve of his suit jacket. When it hit the sun, it sent a sharp beam of light into her eye and she looked away.

"You about to cry? Over that?"

"No. I'm not. I just feel like lately you've been watering down God's word and now I have to be more sensitive to women who dress like men. It makes no sense to me. I thought we were a church."

"Well, see that's the thing. I'm doing a whole rebranding. I'm thinking of calling Vision Church, just Vision or Vision Spiritual Center. It will be a place that accepts people from all walks of life. These Hollywood producers need to hear God's word, too."

"Well, I just feel like you're trying to do anything possible to leave our Pentecostal roots. If you won't stand for something, you'll fall for anything."

"Faith, we're not going to grow the church by being so narrow minded. What do you have against the gays anyway?"

"Nothing! This isn't about them at all! It's about telling men that it's okay that they have a bunch of babies around town with different women just as long as they take care of them. You spoke on that two weeks ago."

"Faith, you got to open your mind or we're going to remain in the past. I'm trying to reach everybody and you just want to reach little old church ladies."

They arrived at the Stellar awards forty minutes later. They were escorted into a VIP area before they walked the red carpet.

Faith could feel that the energy between them had grown distant. She knew that the conversation was far from over and then she received a text while they put on smiles for the cameras while holding hands.

You better act right. The text read.

It sent chills down her spine for the rest of the day. She didn't agree with the direction the church was going in but being a First Lady had been her dream and she had promised to stand by Blake's side through thick and thin. Besides, Blake had no family to speak of. He needed her much more than she needed him right now.

❖

"A Birkin? Baby, no you didn't!" Faith squealed as she slowly opened the package with her new hot pink Birkin by Hermés."

"I sure did! Why wouldn't I buy my First Lady a Birkin?"

Faith has been receiving more gifts from her husband lately and she loved being spoiled but part of her wondered how he had been able to make so much money.

They had just purchased a new building for the church and the overhead cost for maintaining the new location was going to cost them thousands of dollars each month.

However, Blake rarely ever shared their finances with her. Faith was always left in the dark which left her husband in complete control.

"Are you sure we can afford something like this? I don't want to take away from the church."

"Faith, come on now. It's not every day a husband can buy his wife a twenty-thousand- dollar bag. You don't want it? I can take it back."

Faith sighed. Her conscience was bothering her. She loved the purse. It was one of the most beautiful items she had ever owned.

"I can't accept this Blake. I thought we were having trouble paying all our administrative assistants and even the praise dance leader. We also need more stage equipment. I thought we talked about this."

Blake rolled his eyes. "Faith, you're overreacting. All those things will be taken care of. You know what, give me the purse!"

Faith felt a slight burning sensation on her palm as he snatched the purse from her. She watched him throw it on the other lounge chair in their home theatre. The two sat in lounge chairs next to each other while the movie, "White Chicks" played.

She reached over and grabbed the purse. It hurt her that Blake did his best to buy her something so beautiful and she didn't accept it.

"I thought you didn't want it!" Blake fumed.

"I want it, Baby. I want it! I'm sorry. I just never received gifts this special before. I didn't grow up getting stuff like this. My parents worked hard for us but we always had just enough. We never had extra."

Faith moved over to Blake's chair and sat on his lap. She let his long arms wrap around her waist. Clutching her purse, she nuzzled her nose onto his neck like a cat. He gently kissed her forehead. She felt him remove the purse from her hands and then spread her legs so his body was in between them. Their lips met and her body craved more of him each time their tongues merged.

Faith felt the hooks on her bra unclasp. Sweat beads appeared on her skin and she slowly unbuttoned his shirt. She slowly grinded back and forth on his lap. While kissing him, his hands gripped her hips. His Hermés belt confused her at first, but then she found a way to unhook it and began reaching down into his pants. Faith felt his hand stop her from going any lower with all his strength.

She watched him kneel before her while Faith made herself more comfortable in the lounge chair. She spread her legs wide and eventually, his warm tongue gently licked her vagina and then began to suck it. His tongue moved multiple directions just barely touching her clit. Faith gasped and then screamed. She pulled his head closer to her while her fingers slipped through his long curls. His moans vibrated against her thighs. Each time his beard brushed against her legs she bit her tongue.

"Baby, just put it in. I want it," Faith moaned. Tears began streaming down her cheeks. Her legs shook with the slightest touch of his hands.

Blake quickly turned the lights off in the theatre and it was pitch black. She could hear his heavy breathing and then his body pushed her back in the lounge chair. She heard his pants unzip and then his hard penis entered her. Faith groaned and grabbed his body toward hers. She couldn't see him but it turned her on even more.

"You're so beautiful, Baby. I love you," Blake whispered in her ear. She bit her tongue as his teeth scraped her neck, then he sucked it.

After ten minutes of deep strokes, Faith felt her body begin to climax. Her whole body shook and Blake grabbed her and then pulled his body underneath hers. It still hurt because her body had never been penetrated before but each moment lessened the pinching feeling. Eventually, she was too caught up in how good it felt to wonder if she was bleeding.

"Now, I want some kids. Come here," Faith said, pulling his waist toward hers. She reached for his penis, but he pushed her away.

He put himself inside her for a couple more minutes and stroked heavily. He groaned and then pulled himself out as quickly as he could.

"You pulled out?" Faith asked.

"I wasn't thinking. I'm sorry, Baby," Blake said as he disappeared into the bathroom located outside the theatre room.

Faith followed him but Blake slammed the door and locked it before she could. The door almost hit her in the face. "You okay, Baby?" Faith was still recovering. Her body was still moist and sweaty.

"I'm fine. Why are you coming into the bathroom?"

She heard him shuffling around and then turn on the sink. She went into the bedroom to wait on him.

A few minutes later, he glided into the bedroom and laid his head on her shoulder. "I'm sorry, Baby. I was just nervous."

"It's okay, Baby. That was a beautiful first time. I'm even more in love now."

She gently kissed his forehead and relished in the closeness she felt to him. She was finally getting closer to starting her family.

❖

"You're not leading Sunday School anymore?" Faith's mother asked over the phone. Faith was busy putting groceries away to cook one of Blake's favorite meals.

"Well, I'm still going to be involved but I believe that I'm needed elsewhere."

"Faith, you always loved writing and speaking. What else are you going to do?"

"Wherever I'm needed, Mother. My calling isn't just speaking in Sunday School and doing live Bible studies."

Her mother was silent on the phone for so long, Faith forgot they were still on a phone call.

"I've been reading up on Vision Church. You all seem to be leaning more toward the young people. You still Pentecostal?"

"Well, we're moving away from many of the traditions a lot of people are used to."

"I see you're called Vision Spiritual Center now. Are you still a church?"

"I mean technically we are but we accept all religions, genders, and backgrounds."

"I see. I've been listening to your husband's sermons online and he doesn't even preach about what to do or not do anymore. It seems like anything goes. He said something like 'make your heaven on earth' and 'prosperity is God's glory. It's like he believes that the more money you make, the more blessed you are. I thought you two would stick to the Word."

"Mother, we are! You have to reach the people where they are."

"Is that why you have a former gang member, or at

least hope he's former, leading your youth department for young men?"

"We don't judge, Mother. He's turning his life around."

"I thought he was in the news for…never mind. Just don't make everything about money and try to get people saved. Leading God's people is a great responsibility. Always be honest."

"If anyone is honest it's Blake, Mother. I have full trust in him. He's just doing his best to reach out to people that we may not have ever been able to reach before."

"So, y'all don't even call it a church anymore."

"Well, it's a church for some but it's a place to gather for others."

"That doesn't make any sense, Faith. Have you

talked to Tara lately?"

"Mother, let me get going. I have to finish cooking this food before Blake gets home this evening. I love you."

Faith ended the phone call with a swipe of her finger and began placing the raw chicken in flour to prepare to fry her first batch.

She couldn't wait for Blake to get home. Tonight, she planned on trying for a baby again. She had recently gone to the doctor to check on her fertility. Interest in the quality of her eggs had taken over her mind lately. Since she had been so busy with traveling locally with Blake, she had forgotten to open a secure email from her doctor on St. Martin's Medical Offices website that would give her a summary of how fertile she was. Following reading the results, she was supposed to go to her scheduled appointment with her fertility specialist on Friday.

Once she opened her email, she felt blood rush to

her face. She only had a few eggs that were high quality left. Her time was running out much quicker than she expected. She figured if she didn't get pregnant within the next year or two, she might miss her chance. Her doctor was hopeful but she warned Faith that her risk for Down Syndrome, Autism, and other abnormalities were high.

Unfortunately, Blake hadn't even had the decency last time to kick start the baby making process. They had sex, but he had refused to finish inside of her.

She had been tracking her ovulation cycle like a hawk. It was exactly two days before she was scheduled to ovulate which meant she was ripe for reproduction.

Instead of her comfortable bathrobe, Faith slipped on some silk pajamas and wore her sexiest lace bra. The satin robe gently slipped off her shoulders. Her hair was in a slick bun. She hadn't removed any of her makeup and made sure that she brushed on a little more powder when he texted her that he was almost home.

She hadn't been that excited to greet her husband at home in a long time.

Faith was startled when the door opened. Blake's tie was loose around his neck and his eyes were drooping heavily.

She ran toward him and placed her arms around his neck. She kissed him on the lips and removed his jacket.

"What you got all that on for? It's not Valentine's Day," he groaned.

"I made you your favorite meal and I was wondering if we could have a little 'us' time. You've been working hard."

"I'm tired, Faith. I'm not in the mood for anything right now. I'll have to eat later."

Faith felt her blood rushing to her head. "I'm ovulating, Blake! This is the time! My doctor literally just told me that I don't have much time! How long are we going to wait?"

"Are we really going to talk about this right now?" Blake said heading upstairs towards the bedroom.

"Yes! It's almost like you're not attracted to me!" Faith felt her eyes sting with tears.

"I'm not attracted to desperation and that's a fact," Blake said flatly.

He proceeded to walk up the stairs and shook his head. "We have more pressing things to worry about. We have some news outlets calling us some kind of Hollywood cult because we're so popular. Basically, I'm tired. Not tonight."

Faith went back to the kitchen and sobbed so hard, she could barely breathe. Her marriage had been one of the greatest blessings of her life but her regrets were building by the day.

The happy couple everyone saw on the blogs and social media pages were becoming more of a façade. Her mother always told her a man should love a woman more than she loves him. At this point, it seemed like their relationship was completely reliant on the love she gave. She was barely getting anything in return. Faith was married to Blake but Blake was married to Vision Spiritual Center.

Chapter 5

Faith opened her bag from *Bloomingdales* once again to take another sniff of the cologne she bought. It was from the Tom Ford collection and was something Blake had been eyeing for a while. The last time they shopped in the outdoor mall near Beverly Hills, Blake had pointed to a glass case holding the expensive scents.

Once she received her monthly allowance from her husband, Faith dashed back to Beverly Hills to purchase it. Their church anniversary was coming up and she wanted to surprise him. She planned on taking him out to dinner and planning a short, relaxing vacation but, unfortunately, she was married to one of the few men that had everything. Blake was leasing a luxury personal jet he planned to purchase by the end of the year. The couple's spending was beginning to reach into the millions. It was worrying Faith but she wasn't quite sure of how much her husband spent per month. If she asked, he would remind her not to worry about it. She knew that as long as they were financially stable, God was still in the blessing business.

She parked her car and headed inside with her package in hand. Faith always loved wrapping gifts since she was a child so she took out some of her favorite wrapping paper and string. She tried to locate her scissors but she couldn't find them.

Sometimes, she kept scissors in the bathroom but, once she looked in there, she couldn't find them. Thinking back to the last place she saw them, she remembered that Blake had asked for her pair of scissors while he was in the bathroom.

He wasn't home but he had a rule that no one is supposed to use his bathroom. It was an odd rule but she stuck to it because they had gone a while now without an explosive argument.

Carefully, she opened the golden handle to his

private bathroom and went inside. It was usually locked but, this time, she was able to go inside with ease. She checked inside his drawers to find out where the scissors might be. Looking around and listening to see if he was coming in the house, she opened his medicine cabinet. Inside were several medications she didn't recognize. It was a surplus of hormone medication in several boxes. They had all been opened and looked like they had been used daily. Just by looking at the boxes, she couldn't tell what was going on.

Most of the boxes were for hormone therapy. Faith assumed this was one of the reasons Blake was afraid to perform in the bedroom. She wasn't sure but she wanted to have an honest conversation about it. She found needles for injections as well as pills. Her heart dropped knowing all that Blake had done to be normal for her.

Faith hadn't even heard the door open downstairs. Once she exited Blake's bathroom, their eyes met in the hallway that led from the stairs to the master bedroom.

"What were you doing in there?" Blake screamed. Faith had never heard him raise his voice like that before. She almost wanted to run but was frozen in place.

"I was just looking for scissors. Remember I let you borrow my scissors and you never brought them back?"

"Who told you to go in my bathroom?"

Blake ran toward her but then zipped past her shoulder that was blocking the door. The next thing she heard was him punching the wall.

"I'm sorry, Blake. I'm sorry. I didn't think it would make you so upset."

"You took out my medication? Are you crazy? Oh, I'm tired of this shit!"

Faith had never heard her husband use foul language before. "Blake, why do we have to hide things from each other in our marriage?"

156

She watched Blake's shoulders relax. He grabbed his forehead and sighed.

"Look, I need it to grow in my patchy beard. I was embarrassed and didn't want you to think I was less of a man. I used to be skinnier and I got made fun of. I needed to bulk up and I knew this stuff could help me. You looked up what this stuff does online?"

"No. I didn't. I just assumed you were taking them for a male problem of some sort. I wasn't mad. I wanted to be supportive. I am supportive. Why did you hide all this from me?"

"I didn't know what you would say. I was scared that you'd think less of me. I'm always going to have to take this medication for the rest of my life or my beard will be patchy again. You know my beard is part of my brand. Most of the people at Vision are young and beards are what the young people want right now."

"I understand, baby. It's okay," Faith walked toward him and kissed his forehead. Tears were in both their eyes. "I would never judge you."

"You still shouldn't have come in here. I don't know if I can trust you anymore."

"I'm sorry. I should have asked. I just didn't think it was that big of a deal. Men usually don't do much in the bathroom, except shave and shower."

"Well, now you know," Blake said tersely. He turned around and waited for her to leave the bathroom. She did.

He locked the doors and calmly went downstairs.

Faith made him a cup of coffee but silence lingered over them for the rest of the evening. If it was for his beard only, why had it been more of a secret than where the United States held their nuclear weapons?

Faith saw Blake disappear into his office and she turned the coffee maker off. She opened her laptop and decided to dive into her social media timeline. There was a trend going around called the "#BabytoBaeChallenge" where participants were supposed to post a baby picture next to a picture of them where they're fully grown.

She loved to participate in these challenges and dug through the digital photo albums on her phone to find some of her oldest pictures. After a few minutes, she finally found a picture of herself as a baby. It had been scanned years ago when she first began to make online profiles. As soon as she was about to post it to her social media page, she saw that there were a few married couples that had posted their baby pictures side by side and then their baby pictures underneath.

Faith wanted to join in so she scoured her desktop to see if Blake had given her pictures of what he looked like when he was a baby. She had none. The oldest pictures she could find were of when he had first come to

California. There weren't many and she could use them but that would have defeated the purpose of the challenge.

It was still tension in the air so Faith was afraid to knock on Blake's office door. However, she felt that it was such a simple request that he shouldn't get mad at her. She had already gone down to his first picture on his social media profile and he had no childhood pictures. There were also no pictures of his family. Everything was Bible quotes, a short video of him preaching, or a selfie of him wearing one of his favorite outfits.

"Blake," Faith said, slowly opening his door.

"Yes? What?"

She slowly opened his door wider and put one foot inside.

"Baby," she said, touching his left shoulder. "Would you happen to have any baby pictures?"

Blake was answering emails and listening to an audio of T.D. Jakes, one of his greatest preaching inspirations.

"Why?"

"I just wanted to have it. I saw this cute little social media challenge and I wanted to participate."

"A challenge about what?"

Faith could tell annoyance was growing in his voice.

"It was a baby to adult challenge. I thought it would be cute to put our baby pictures up next to how we look now."

"You do that?"

The scorn in Blake's voice made her feel like she

could have turned red all over if she was lighter.

"I mean, it was just cute. I'm sure the people haven't seen you as a baby yet."

"I don't need them to. Besides, I don't have any," he said with a drop in his voice. "They all burned up in a fire."

Faith's eyes grew wide. "A fire? All your pictures?"

"All of them," he said flatly. "That's why I don't have any of me. It's not my fault."

Faith covered her mouth and sat on his lap. "Blake, Baby. You didn't tell me you were the victim of a fire when you were a child. Everyone made it out, right?"

"Yeah, we all made it out. It was a disaster. I don't like to think about it. I hate that I have no memories of when I was little."

She rubbed his forehead and kissed it. "I'm so sorry, Baby. None of your other relatives kept any pictures of you? What about your grandmother?"

"My family's always been so split up. My mother had issues with her mother. Of course, I'm not close to my family. I have no siblings. My mother passed and I don't know that much about my father."

"Well, Baby we make a family. A beautiful one. This is why you need a baby of your own."

"I think that's why I'm hesitant. I had so many issues with family growing up that I don't want one myself. I think it's a defense mechanism. I mean, I do want one but I always think about losing the child or you. I don't know. I hate talking about all this. God is still good, though. He's brought me through. I'm sorry I don't have any pictures, baby."

"No, baby. It's okay. I didn't know all that. Look, forget the challenge. It doesn't matter."

Faith let him push his head into her breasts. She let his soft hair part between her fingers. One of her favorite physical qualities on Blake was his hair. She hoped her children took his curly hair at least. She had envisioned having a little girl with long ponytails down her back that never needed to be permed or pressed.

While sitting peacefully on his lap she kept thinking about how much it hurt Blake that he had no contact with his family. He had never expressed wanting to find them but Faith was determined to get his family back in his life. She felt like it might soften his heart to have a family of his own. She calmly thought about hiring a private investigator or doing the research on her own. She had heard of people meeting their fathers and mothers for the first time using social media. Blake would certainly refuse to take an ancestry test to link him to relatives, so all she had to rely on were clues in the house.

He had a file cabinet where he kept many of his important papers so she would start there. Faith felt like she had to know his roots. Who would her children be related to? Blake was one of the most transparent pastors online. He was open about his life, his marriage, and how he studied God's word but he had no identity beyond from when they met. For the sake of her future family, she needed to know. What kind of wife didn't know anything about her husband? This was beyond baby pictures.

After Blake went to sleep, Faith began searching online for anyone with his last name. She scoured social media for other McPhersons but each one she found was white or didn't appear to have any connection to Blake. She messaged all the Blake McPhersons but, once she received messages back, none of them knew a Blake.

The evening got darker and Faith's eyes grew heavier but she attempted to do a people search online for Blake McPherson. He appeared on *Google* as a pastor but not anywhere else. There were two other Blake

McPhersons but they were White.

She paid for a background check for the person named Blake who had the same address, was the same age, and the same race as her husband. She was sure it was him. The background check was supposed to be instant so she could get his past addresses and phone numbers. She would also be able to see if anyone was connected to him.

Before paying, she couldn't find anyone that was a family member linked to him. Previously, when she had searched for other people, they would have several addresses and family members linked to their name. It was strange that Blake had none but she hoped that a simple background check would result in a few names linked to him. She knew the risk she was staking because Blake might become furious but she was determined to bring him back together with his family.

Within an hour, the report had come back. She felt sweat slide down the sides of her body and her heartbeat could be felt in her throat.

Blake McPherson existed but he had no history before three years ago. It was as if Blake had just appeared on earth three years ago. He only had one other address in Los Angeles which was the same one he had when they first met. He was linked to no family members or any companies.

Faith was beginning to panic. How was her husband unable to have any connections to anyone outside of the people he knew in Los Angeles? There was no birth certificate available or any work history. She wondered if he had changed his name. He could have had a criminal history he was trying to wipe out. Faith had never felt that he could have done any heinous crime or been in a gang. He could be aggressive but he was no criminal that was going out of his way to hurt people.

Since her search turned up nothing, she felt a sense of defeat. At best, she had nothing to worry about and it was probably for the best that he didn't have contact with his kin. She wondered if they had been some crime family that he had tried his best to distance himself from. Blake could be so secretive sometimes that she didn't think it was such a far-fetched idea. In the morning, when Blake would board his plane to Texas to meet with Joel Osteen, she would get to work searching through every file he had in his office. Their whole existence could be part of some crime scheme, and Faith would technically be an accomplice.

She said a long prayer, took a shower, and lay in the bed for an hour with her eyes closed. Her heart longed for her heavenly father to protect her. It was past just searching for a long, lost family at this point.

Faith woke up at the crack of dawn. She hadn't even felt Blake lie down to sleep next to her. He had left close to 4 A.M. that morning to catch the private jet that Joel Osteen had sent to pick him up. Not having a plane had been one of Blake's biggest gripes lately. Faith didn't see that point in having a private jet at their disposal. She hated small aircrafts but Blake was more concerned with keeping up with the wealthy than she was.

She still had her pajamas on and crept into Blake's office. The cold, wooden floor kept shocking the warm temperature of her feet. The office was downstairs next to the music room.

It was locked.

Later, she found out his bathroom was too.

Faith was tired of being locked out of rooms in her own house. Blake shouldn't have had anything to hide. Back in her room, she opened her laptop to view Blake's background check again. She wondered if she had missed something. As she scraped through the document, she saw nothing more than what had already been exposed. Blake had as much information on him as what would have been available in a phone book.

Feeling defeated, she laid out her clothes to head to

the First Ladies brunch she was hosting as a restaurant in the late morning. She hated that her life had become a lot of fake smiling and greeting women that secretly envied her. It was like living in the Real Housewives reality show but for church ladies. Since she and Tara had fallen out, she had very few women that she could go to for a real conversation that spoke to her soul. The same Bible quotes over and over were beautiful but it seemed like everyone around her was trying to look as Christian as possible without living as a Christian woman. Part of her missed having her own career and identity.

Now, she was just Bishop McPherson's wife. Elegant, ladylike, and a role model to all other young women in the church. However, she was just his wife and she felt her voice in the church being less significant than the day before.

As long as she made him happy and looked pretty, she was doing her job.

Faith was running late for church. She loved to be in the house of God but lately, she had been feeling sluggish. Blake usually went without her. He was usually driven to the church in his silver Bentley that he had just purchased. Faith still preferred to drive herself. It just didn't sit right with her to be catered to all the time.

Thankfully, she had her mink eyelashes already installed so she didn't have to worry about mascara. However, once she placed her lipstick on, she had no time to finish up her eyeliner and even find her most comfortable bra. She left the house with a red skirt and white blouse. Her thin Gucci purse hit her right hip as she slipped on her black stilettos.

She was supposed to be teaching Sunday School that morning and hoped that people would wait around for another fifteen minutes. Once she was out the door, she had forgotten to take off her headscarf. She ran back in to brush her hair out and let the curls fall toward her shoulders. Luckily, her hair was already done so she didn't have to do much to it for it to be presentable.

Faith took the Prius to church and parked in her reserved spot. Blake's Phantom was already parked in his spot closest to the back of the church. Blake had his own entrance. He usually sat in his office until it was time for him to preach.

Once she got out of her car, she felt a vibration from her phone. Blake had texted her.
See me.

Although it was a short text, Faith read it as aggressive. If he had something to say to her, she would have preferred he sent it over text. Her women's Sunday School segment was going to start soon and he was going to make her even more late than she already was.

The balls of her feet hurt as she tried to rush to his

office. The marble floors inside had the sound of her heels that tapped against the marble echoing throughout the hallway.

When she reached Blake, he had his hands clasped against his chest. His eye contact was on the mystery woman in front of him.

Faith's heart began pounding.

"Yes?" She said meekly.

"I'll make this short, Sweetheart. From now on, Jessie Madison is going to be leading the Women's Sunday School."

Faith knew Jessie Madison as one of the leading women in Vision Spiritual Center. She was also a lesbian and had just gotten married the previous summer. She was younger and more active on social media. She was also more masculine and wore male clothing that had been tailored to fit her slim body. Faith and Jessie Madison's eyes never met. Faith knew that if she looked at her, the tears might well up quicker.

Faith had truly enjoyed Sunday School. It was one of her outlets but because she wasn't "liberal" enough or younger than thirty-five, she was dragging the whole program down.

"Don't think it's anything against you, Baby. We just need to switch it up. Jessie will be an excellent addition to the team."

"Understood," Faith said under her breath. "I have to get to service. I'll see both of you soon."

Faith stood and paced down the hallway. She swore steam was coming out of her ears. Once she opened her car door, she let the tears flow. Nothing that she did was ever good enough for Blake. Every time she got somewhat comfortable, he wanted to shut her down. Vision Spiritual Center was becoming a foreign place. From the music to the teaching, she felt out of the loop.

Her phone began vibrating several times. She knew it was Blake calling her but she needed some time to get her thoughts together. Faith went to a coffee shop and decided to order some tea before the start of the first church service. She knew Blake hated when she didn't answer her phone so she decided to finally answer. Once she looked at her texts, she saw that they had become increasingly aggressive. He even began to accuse her of talking to Cameron.

Cameron seemed more level headed anyway. Since he was always accusing her of talking to him, maybe this time she would take him up on it.

Faith found Cameron's number and called. Since her relationship with her mother and Tara had been strained lately, he seemed like a perfect plan b.

The hot berry tea calmed her nerves, and then he

picked up on the third ring.

"Hey, Faith! How's everything going? I passed by women's Sunday School this morning and didn't see you. You feeling well?"

"I'm well. That's actually what I called you about. Bishop took me down as the main speaker and replaced me with Jessie Madison. I was wondering if you two had a meeting about this."

"No, we didn't. I've never been a fan of hers. I think he just wants someone younger to attract all the teens and young people joining the church. I heard you were wonderful though. I'm surprised he's switching up. What are you going to do now?"

"Sit there and look pretty. That's all I can do."

"I'll talk to him."

"No! It's okay. Where are you? Are you inside the

church?"

"I'm actually in Bishop McPherson's office. He's not here though. We had a finance meeting scheduled."

Her heart sank.

"Are you sure you don't want me to talk to him?"

Faith was silent on the phone.

"Who are you talking to?"

Blake's voice was so loud, it felt like the phone's receiver was at his mouth.

"It's Faith. We were just..."

"That's Faith? Tell her to see me after church immediately!"

"Uh, Bye Faith." Cameron abruptly ended the call.

Faith felt like she wanted to throw up in her mouth.

I knew you were cheating on me! You gonna need the Lord on your side when I get done with you!

Faith turned her phone off and went home.

It felt strange to her to not attend church that morning. All morning long until the afternoon, she waited to hear Blake's wrath once he entered their home. The one thing he asked of her was her loyalty. She had given him that, but it seemed like Cameron was the only person that was willing to hear her side of the story. Her own husband was starting to reduce any leadership she had in the church. She expected many of the church members to not take her side but it cut her deeply that her own husband wanted to reduce her to being the old lady in the church that everyone ignored.

She looked in the mirror and pulled at her face. She opened her eyes wide and stretched them to see if she could find any strange moles or wrinkles. There were a few more strands of gray in her hair since the last time she had it colored. Faith wondered if it was her appearance that was pulling her further away from youth. She tried to dress as youthful as she could but it was to no avail.

The afternoon turned into the evening and Faith waited for Blake to return. She could barely sit and relax anywhere in the house. He hadn't texted her which was unlike him. They usually kept in contact more often on Sundays so they could coordinate.

It was 9 P.M. when Faith heard the door open and the pungent smell of alcohol drifted into the door. She almost thought someone had broken in because she and Blake never had alcohol in the house.

She went into the living room to make sure it was him at the door and he stumbled in the room. His knees buckled underneath him.

"Blake? Are you drunk? What happened?"

Faith grabbed her husband's shoulders and then ran to the kitchen to splash water on his face from the faucet.

When she returned, his fist came toward her but missed. Faith screamed and jumped on the couch.

"Where were you?" She shrieked. "Why were you drinking?"

"You drove me to this point, Faith! You're in love with Cameron. No one loves me!"

"Blake, you've been irrational lately. I think it's time to take a break."

She planned on telling his executives that he was

cancelling all meeting for the next two days.

He stood once more and then his body fell to the wooden floor with a thud. She touched his chest to feel his heart beating. Blake gasped for air. The scent of the alcohol he had consumed surrounded her.

She let him lay there until the next morning and locked the bedroom door. It was hard for her to fall asleep but then she remembered that in his slumber, he more than likely had his file cabinet keys.

Tiptoeing around him she grabbed his keys from inside his jacket. When she reached his office, she locked the door behind her.

The file cabinet was miraculously unlocked. She turned on the light and dug through the files looking for anything with his name on it. She found an old phonebook with different numbers inside. Opening it, there was a number listed as "Mama" and then remembered that Blake had talked about how sick she was. It was possible that she had passed on. He had another number listed as "Big Sis" but Blake had said several times that he didn't have any siblings.

She had brought her phone with her so she took pictures of the two numbers but then went back to searching through the cabinets trying to find anything else hinting at his background.

There was a file folder that had the outline of what looked like was a social security card. It had his name on it as "Blake McPherson." The birth certificate was so faded, she wasn't able to make out anything. There was a name that started with a "B" where his was, but she was unable to tell if that was his birth certificate or someone else's. It looked like it had been intentionally destroyed or placed in water.

Faith put everything back in the file cabinet and unlocked the door. She headed downstairs and saw that

Blake was still in the same position she left him in.

Opening his wallet, she found nothing strange. She placed a blanket on him and tip toed back upstairs.

She turned on the shower and let the hot water soak into her body. Her mind couldn't stop thinking about the two numbers she found. There was a chance that they weren't working and then her search would have to start all over again. Faith hoped to exhaust as many of her options as she could before she resorted to hiring a private investigator. Faith was sure that God was going to lead her to the answer in her own house.

She still had love for her husband but tolerating him every day had become a hassle. There was no way that the man she married would have resorted to heavy drinking.

It was as if Blake was doing anything he could to put blame on her. If it wasn't that she was talking to

Cameron, she wasn't good enough to speak in church. She felt that she was becoming less of a prop and more of her husband's shadow. She had no identity outside of him. She used to love going to church but she dreaded Sunday morning every week.

Blake was holding on to some dark secret and her intuition was telling her that she was close to solving it. Faith didn't believe in divorce so she hoped that they would be able to work through a criminal past or even infidelity. To her, there was still a lovable man behind the mask he showed to the people.

As of now, there would be only one way to get her husband back and that was to find out the truth.

Chapter 6

The next day, Faith felt sore all over her body. She had attempted to pull Blake onto the rug because she thought he looked uncomfortable in his drunken sleep. Once it felt like she was about to dislocate her shoulder, she left him alone.

Faith heard him shuffling around in the morning but he never entered their bedroom. He had another closet and his own bathroom, so she knew he would have been able to find clothing if he planned on leaving.

She looked at her texts. He hadn't sent anything to her. For about forty-five minutes, she could hear him taking a shower and then his shoes tapping against their hardwood floor. Her whole body tensed up with each step he took.

Eventually, the main door slammed and Faith finally opened the bedroom door to see if he was gone. The lingering scent of alcohol remained in the air. She went to sit on the couch in their den and breathed a heavy sigh of relief.

Then, she remembered the phone numbers she found from his file cabinet last night. Since she didn't know when he would come back, she decided it would be best to do her research in a safer place. The local community college's library had study pods which she could reserve for an hour.

After showering and slipping on a comfortable sweat suit, Faith put her hair up and headed out the door with no makeup on.

The ride over to the college was short, but it seemed like an eternity. Once she reserved the study pod, she locked the door behind her. It had glass walls, but she preferred it to anywhere else because it was sound proof.

Faith dialed the first phone number of the woman that had been listed as "Mother." The moistness from her palms almost made the phone slip out of her hands.

It went to voicemail. There was no voice that asked her to leave a message. Hoping she was contacting the right person, she said that she was wondering if she had reached the mother of Blake McPherson.

She called the other number, but the person did not pick up and their voicemail box was full. She texted the number, hoping it was a cellphone.

Hello, my name is Faith McPherson. I'm married to Blake McPherson, and I had a few questions.

The number from "Mother" popped up on her screen.

Faith answered it on the first ring.

"Hello?" the other voice said. "Who is this?"

"My name is Faith McPherson. I found your number in my husband's things listed as 'Mother.' Are you the mother of Blake McPherson?"

"Blake who? I don't know no Blake."

The woman had a soft southern accent that didn't sound as sickly as Faith had expected.

"Oh, well maybe this number was changed. I found it in my husband's things and I've been trying to find his birth mother for a while. I was just holding out hope that I had finally found her."

"No, honey. I don't know any Blake. I don't have any sons. I only have daughters. My eldest hasn't spoken to me in years. I don't know where she is."

Faith felt like she wanted to end the conversation

but something told her to ask the woman more questions.

"I'm so sorry your daughter left. I couldn't imagine not communicating with my mother."

Faith felt a heaviness in her heart after she said that because Blake had done nothing but pull her away from her mother because she was calling Vision Spiritual Center a cult.

"Well, I'm sorry about that, Ma'am."

"But, maybe you can help me. Where are you from?"

"I live in Los Angeles, California."

"From what I last heard, Bianca ran to California. I don't know for sure. Do you mind if I send a picture of her. Maybe you've seen her."

Faith could feel the pain in the woman's voice. She wanted to be able to help her if she could.

"Yes Ma'am, I could do that. Send me the picture."

"Wait, let me get my daughter, Sophia, to send it through my phone."

After two minutes, Faith felt a buzz as the picture came in.

The woman in the picture was beautiful. She was light skinned with long hair pulled into a long braid. She wasn't wearing any makeup, and the clothes she wore looked masculine.

"She was a tomboy, huh?" Faith said, trying to chuckle.

"She was a lesbian. A dyke lesbian, too. I told her I wasn't comfortable with that lifestyle. I really wasn't comfortable with my daughter acting like and looking like a man."

Faith found out the woman's name was Mary, and she was from Detroit. She had two daughters, Sophia and Bianca, but her eldest, Bianca, ran to California after a dispute and was never heard from again.

Faith studied the picture carefully and noticed that the woman had bright, green eyes and the same birthmark on her neck. It was a mark that almost looked like an Irish Shamrock on their collarbone.

"You want me to add you on social media? I have so many more pictures of her on there. She was such a beautiful girl and I miss her so much. I've put up "Missing" posters all over my area but nothing has come up. Her picture went viral once but nothing came of it. I know you're a stranger but hopefully you could spread the word in California. I really need to know what happened to my child. I can't leave this earth without knowing. My heart is telling me that she's still alive."

"We'll find her, Ma'am. I'm sure we will. She was a beautiful girl. She almost reminds me of someone I know but I can't really put my finger on it."

"Thank you for helping me. I know God will allow me to find my child."

Once they ended the conversation, Faith felt a wave of emotions throughout her body. She couldn't believe that this person she called was in such a desperate situation. Although her daughter was not a child, she knew there was no greater pain than not knowing where your child is.

Faith left the study pod and drove home. She figured that Bianca and Blake were siblings. Blake and Bianca probably had different fathers. She and Blake looked exactly alike.

Blake said he had no siblings but he probably wasn't counting the kids that were from other women.

Faith had just received a text from Blake.

Where are you?

I was just at the mall. I'm coming home now.

Come home. I got to talk about something. It's about the church.

On her way there, Faith looked at her phone at the stoplight. She saw a text pop up from Cameron.
Did you see this?

He sent her an article on Blake being accused of groping women at Vision Center.

No, I hadn't.

I don't know if it's true. But, I don't plan on coming back. It's going to get really ugly if more women come out with accusations.

Faith's heart was beating fast. The article was titled, "*Popular Spiritual Leader Accused of Sex Abuse.*"

She wanted to read the article but she was almost home. She had gotten a ticket before for having her phone in her hand while driving.

Once she arrived at their condo, Faith barely wanted to get out of the car. She scrolled down her social media and saw everyone posting about it. The church's social media page had been swarmed with people wanting to know what happened. She didn't see anyone talking negatively yet. Faith texted their social media manager and asked her to close the comment sections on all Vision Spiritual Center's pages.

Thank you! Pastor has already alerted me. She texted back.

Faith ran into their home as quickly as her feet could take her. Once her key unlocked the door, she saw

Blake with his head in his hands. His legs were shaking and he refused to look up.

She wrapped her arms around his neck and kissed his forehead. All of a sudden, the rising fear she had felt after she left the study pod had dissipated. All she could think about was protecting her husband who was now facing the greatest fights of his life.

"Baby, I know you didn't do anything. They know we've been pretty successful lately and they want to extort us. This too shall pass."

His sobs were almost unbearable. She had never felt so sorry for someone in her life. Faith knew this wasn't the best time to admit that she had spoken to his possible step-mother or the mother of his long-lost sister.

"They're going to take down everything I've built! I never touched those women."

Faith read the news article while she caressed him. There were not over fifteen accusers all telling the same story. They were all accusing Blake of touching them inappropriately during private meetings about church business. Shockwaves ran through her body when she saw that there were at least two underage males that claimed they had been groped by Blake as well.

"They won't take us down, Babe. It's not true so they won't prevail. See, these are the times when I wish you had more honest people around you. You need more family around."

Blake remained silent and continued sniffling into his coat.

Faith stood to make him some tea and turned her phone off. "You should block most people from your phone. I see your phone just going off. Just turn it off for now."

She watched slowly reach for his phone and then

throw it across the room. The screen shattered and pieces of glass hit the corner of the room. Blake disappeared into his office for the rest of the evening. Faith decided that she would write a message to the social media manager for damage control.

She hated when Blake shut down. Faith had tried to get marriage counseling both online and offline but Blake consistently refused.

It felt like her world was tumbling down faster than she could have ever imagined. She knew it would be best to give Blake space for the time being. It was likely that he had sent word to his board of ministers that he would be out on Sunday.

Faith opened her laptop again to check her social media and noticed that Mary had added her as a friend. She accepted the request and then immediately scanned the woman's page for clues.

As expected, the woman had various pictures of her

lost daughter from when she was a baby until her early thirties. It puzzled Faith why a young woman would lose contact with her family so late in life.

Mary had created multiple "Missing" posters to find her daughter, one of which had been shared ten-thousand times.

Faith saw a strong resemblance between Bianca and Blake. They shared the same smile, same smirk, and love of church. It appeared as if Bianca had been immersed in her local church since she was a child. There were several pictures of her as a teenager standing at the podium to speak on monthly Youth Days.

It was possible the young woman had been kidnapped and killed. There was a lot of human trafficking going on in the news so Bianca could have gotten caught up with that. Faith was surprised that the police hadn't been able to find a trace but, since she was a Black girl, she knew that the media weren't always interested in finding missing African Americans.

Blake entered the room again to refill his coffee cup. Faith immediately closed her laptop with a startle.

"You alright?" He asked.

"I'm fine. Are you okay?"

"I'll be okay. I'm innocent until proven guilty. This whole 'Me Too' situation is starting to seep into the churches now. You got to be my prayer warrior, Baby."

Faith felt her heart soften. "I will, Baby. I'll be praying for you. We'll get through this."

Blake nodded his head and went upstairs with tears on the rim of his eyes.

Faith reopened her laptop and wondered if she would ever be able to get the image of Bianca out of her head.

❖

The media circus had become a nightmare for Faith. It seemed like everyone was against her husband. He still had quite a few supporters left as she could see online. Most of the negative commentary had been erased by their quick social media team.

Because of the backlash, Blake had sold even more books and had received more views on their videos. Faith's family and marriage podcast had suddenly become more popular.

Faith stayed home that Sunday but she watched Blake make his way to Vision Spiritual Center. He wore a muted gray suit, a red tie, and combed his hair backward.

She noticed that his eyes were more sunken in. His athletic shoulders were slumped forward.

"Maybe I should go," Faith whispered.

"No," he said, brushing her hand away from his shoulder. "I don't want you in this. It'll be media everywhere. I got to do what I gotta do to get my church back. I'm not expecting a large turnout, but I've accepted that fact."

"I'm just really proud that you're being so brave."

Her heart sank as he nodded his head and exited out their door. She caressed his shoulders again. He hadn't been eating well lately, so his shoulders seemed narrower than usual.

Faith stayed glued to her laptop for the rest of the morning to watch the livestream. She couldn't see the audience that clearly but she saw many familiar faces.

Blake didn't arrive at the sanctuary until the end of the service. He was met with loud applause which surprised Faith. He had invited a Rabbi and a Buddhist monk to accompany him in the pulpit. Each of them prayed for him and asked God to protect him. It was a solemn ceremony that had very little music. Faith knew he was doing the best he could to re-consecrate himself in front of the people. Faith saw that the comments on the livestream were mainly positive. Blake seemed in better spirits but once the camera panned back out, it was only about five hundred people in the crowd when they had formerly boasted almost two thousand.

Hollywood had become rampant with sexual abuse cases and no one in the industry wanted to have their career associated with a predator. Vision Center had mainly attracted musicians, actors, producers, and directors over the time they had been open. The only people that stayed were there out of curiosity or because they truly believed in Vision Spiritual Center's unique doctrine.

"You can do this, Baby," Faith whispered to the computer screen with a cup of tea in her hand.

There were still dozens of articles from popular Christian blogs accusing Blake of all kinds of abuse. Faith recognized some of the women that had spoken up had been involved in the youth and music department. She had trained many of those women.

She scrolled down her social media timeline and saw that the Los Angeles Times had done an exclusive article with Jessie Madison. She was the woman that had taken over her Sunday School segment.

Apparently, Blake used to push himself against her in his office and try to kiss her. Once, he threatened to put a piece of fruit from his desk up her vagina.

She claimed that he never revealed his penis to her but he asked to give her oral sex on more than one occasion.

The article was becoming too graphic for her to read. She didn't want to believe that it was her husband that had been cheating on her all this time. Not only did he cheat, he was a sexual predator on the loose. There was a high chance that he could end up in jail for years and they might lose everything they worked for. Everything Faith had was tied to him. She had no money or property of her own. They had been spending money like water falling out of their hands. Sunday's offering was not going to cover most of their major expenses if only a few hundred people came.

Faith was frozen in fear. She disappeared into her bedroom and changed into more comfortable clothes. She refused to do anything but sit in silence for the rest of the afternoon until Blake came home.

Was he actually going to end up in somebody's jail and who was this Bianca?

It still seemed like the wrong time to ask but Faith thought she would try to bring the question up anyway. She figured that Blake would be in much better spirits after a successful service. Faith was sure he would come home with tons of ideas on how to rebuild their congregation. They would have to start from square one unless the law got involved.

Faith continued scrolling on her social media timeline. She had blocked anyone that had anything negative say about Vision Spiritual Center. She saw that Mary had posted another "Missing" poster of Bianca Mackenzie. Faith shared it and, two minutes later, she saw that Mary had sent her an Emoji of two hands clasped together to thank her.

How do you know about her? Blake texted several minutes later.

Faith had forgotten that she had posted on her regular account and not her church account that Blake wasn't following.

Blake came home an hour later. He usually stayed after church for meetings but arrived at home as soon as possible. Faith met him at the door once she heard his keys.

He was somber but she hugged him as tightly as she could and kissed him on the forehead. "It'll get better, baby. We can do this."

"I want to know what you know about Bianca," Blake said with his right eye twitching. Faith felt a sinking feeling in her chest.

"I just shared the picture online. I didn't know her but I felt bad for the mother and wanted to help her out."

Blake began to shed a waterfall of tears. Faith noticed that he began to breathe heavily and almost fell into her arms as if he had been hurt.

"Bianca is my twin sister. I don't know where she is. We could never find her. I don't want to speak about her ever again. Her mother hated her. There's no use looking for her. She doesn't want to be found."

His words cut through Faith's heart like a knife.

She could feel how deep his pain was for his sister.

"Look, her mother is crazy. Have you been in contact with her?"

Suddenly, his voice became shaky.

"I...I just sent her a message saying that I was praying for her. I mean we should be praying for those that are missing. Shouldn't we?"

"Don't contact her anymore," Blake said sharply. He raised his palm to her face.

"I won't, Baby. I won't. I just want you to get some rest."

She noticed that Blake had not been himself lately but it appeared as if the sex abuse allegations were beginning to take him over the edge.

His phone kept ringing several times in a row. She knew it was possibly the media. They now knew where they lived and someone sent a text to him that a news van was parked outside their complex because they wanted to interview them.

Faith refused to go outside for the rest of the afternoon for fear that she would get ambushed by a reporter. She had hoped the news cycle would eventually forget their story but it had been three days and the interest was growing. At that point, her biggest fear was how they would be able to live off just the savings they had. Blake and Faith together had been able to acquire many expenses such as their five cars, their condo and mansion in Malibu, the private jet Blake had just recently purchased, and their various charities in Africa and India that still needed money to run.

Their books were beginning to sell more because of the scandal but Faith feared that a "tell-all" book would overtake the sales of their devotionals and inspirational books eventually. Jessie Madison seemed like she was out for blood. She had done the majority of the interviews on television.

While Bianca was flipping channels that evening, she caught Jessie Madison being interviewed by Oprah for a Sunday Night special.

"I don't know, Ms. Winfrey. Something was just off about that man. It was like being in a cult. But something else was just personally off with him. I had never been able to put my finger on it."

"Was he possibly bisexual or gay?"

"Probably. I'm not sure. I just know that I had to get out of that church."

Faith turned the TV off as quickly as she could get her hand on the remote.

She had meant to turn her phone off but then heard a text come through.

It was Mary again.

I just wanted to thank you for sharing my daughter's picture. You've been the only California person I've known that's at least attempted to help me out.

You're very welcome. No problem.

I don't know who to tell this to but God told me that my child is in California. I received a vision about it last night. He told me that she isn't far from you.

Faith furrowed her brows and shook her head. The lady's search for her missing daughter had reduced her to insanity.

I know you're a prayer warrior. I see you're in the church. Are you married?

I am.

Well then can both of you pray that I find my child in Los Angeles? My heart is telling me she's been kidnapped.

Faith wanted to tell her that Bianca wasn't a child and that she probably left home on her own terms. She could have left due to abuse or just a simple disagreement she had with her mother over her lesbian lifestyle.

I'll keep praying, Mary.

"Who are you texting back and forth?"

Blake had his arms folded in the corner of the kitchen where Faith stood.

"Cameron?"

"No."

"That lady from Facebook?"

"No. I'm not!"

"I told you to stop talking to random people on the internet. What is wrong with you?"

Faith tried to step backward as Blake pulled at her arm to get her phone. He threw the phone across the kitchen and she shivered inside when his hands turned into closed fists.

"I'm not gon' hit you. I'm in enough trouble as it is. I'm in need of support and here you go talking to people who want to tear us apart. Next thing I know, you'll be going to the media."

"But, Baby. You had such a good day on Sunday. You had the Rabbi and Buddhist Monk speak for you and re-consecrate you in front of the people. We still have a loyal few hundred on our side. We still have a fairly large church."

Faith's neck stretched forward as he grabbed her chin forcefully. She could tell he had been smoking cigarettes. "Don't trust anyone. We only got each other. You hear me. This isn't over. Jessie Madison is a liar. She's one of the false prophets that the Bible talks about. She or anyone else is not to be trusted. Block all your social media and all your phone numbers. We're going to have to ride this out."

Faith could hear Blake's phone vibrating from his pocket.

"It's my lawyer," he said.

The conversation went on for five minutes but it seemed like an eternity. The tears collecting at the rim of his eyes let her know that it wasn't good.

She later found out that he was going to have to be questioned and then eventually go to court. Faith heard the lawyer tell Blake that Jessie Madison had voice recordings, DNA evidence on her underwear, and hundreds of inappropriate texts that had come from him. Not only would he lose his church, he would most likely lose his status as a free man and Faith felt like throwing up knowing she might be going down with him.

"I'm going out. I gotta go talk to my lawyer."

Faith stood in front of the door.

"Blake, there's media everywhere. We should just lay low until all this passes over."

"I got to do something. I'm not gonna let these people take over my church. How are we going to survive?"

"Blake, look. Maybe it's time we just focus on our books and our social media presence. I feel like all of this is spinning out of control."

Faith watched Blake's bottom lip begin to tremble. "See, I thought you were on my side."

"I am! I'm your wife! I don't want to lose the church but Jessie Madison is saying all these crazy, outlandish things that aren't true. She was talking to Oprah for God's sake! How do we compete with that? We should salvage what we have now so we don't lose everything."

The door almost swung in Faith's face and hit her. Blake stormed over to the elevator. She feared for the worst because she knew he might be bombarded with the media that had been parked on their street just waiting to catch a glimpse of the famed pastor and his wife.

Faith had been ordering in food or using an alternate exit with large sunglasses on if the security guard on duty that day allowed it.

She wondered if any of the medicine she saw in the cabinet that one time was affecting his mood. Faith was sure that she had seen a bottle marked "steroid." Once, his muscle tone had been much more apparent before he stopped eating as much. The sexual abuse allegations had made Blake eat as little a few crackers a day.

Faith picked her phone up from the floor. The protective glass screen was shattered but it was fine. She saw she had missed a few texts from Cameron.

Almost as soon as she lifted her eyes from the screen, a phone call came through.

It was Blake's lawyer.

"Hello? Is this Faith McPherson?"

"Yes, it is."

"Your husband never arrived and I keep calling him. I've tried texting him but he won't answer. Do you think you could get through? This is very unlike him."

"Yes. I'm going to call him immediately."

Faith ended the phone call and attempted calling Blake multiple times. He finally picked up after she called him ten consecutive times.

"I'm parked on the side of the freeway," he began. "I'm about to swallow all these pills. I got a twenty-two to my head right now. I can't do this."

Faith wanted to scream but she remained calm. "Blake, everything will be okay. Please, listen to me. Don't do this. I love you. I love you."

Faith put him on mute and called 911 on their house phone which they rarely used.

"Help! My husband is trying to kill himself on the side of the 10 freeway. Help me!"

She fell to her knees and said every prayer her brain could compute. Faith felt like her body was frozen but she ran to the underground parking garage to speed over the nearest freeway onramp hoping she could find him.

There were media trucks along the sidewalk. She was temporarily blinded by camera flashes as she pulled out of the parking lot. It almost made her run into a photographer.

She arrived at the freeway within minutes. Helicopters were flying overhead. There was heavy traffic so she parked her car as close to the freeway as she could and ran toward the onramp.

A policeman blocking the onramp stopped.

"Please! That's my husband! Please! His name is Blake McPherson. I need to see my husband!"

He stepped aside and let her through.

❖

At the hospital, Blake had denied that Faith or anyone else came into the room with him. He had swallowed too many of the pills in his hand and had to have his stomach pumped.

Cameron and one other church associate had made it to the hospital. Once Faith saw Cameron, she embraced him.

"He won't let me see him. What do you think that's all about?" Faith said. "I'm going up there. I'll let you all know how he's doing."

Faith walked to the front desk and asked if she could get her husband's room number. She said that she was his wife and they gave it to her. The receptionist that denied her access had gone on break so she decided to ask the other lady that had taken her place.

She took the elevator to the tenth floor and tried her best to move past the doctors and nurses that were looking past her. She approached his room but was stopped by the nurse that had just walked out.

"Sister?" The nurse asked.

"No, his wife."

The nurse's eye grew big. "Oh, well um. You can come in."

Faith slid past the nurse. Blake was facing the other direction so he didn't see her come in. She picked up the doctor's clipboard as quietly as she could. It was covered with a blank sheet of paper. Immediately, she noticed that the entire document had a faint word that read "Confidential."

She quickly scanned the document to read what type of medication he had taken. It looked like he had swallowed several Xanax and Percocet pills at once with alcohol in his system. There was a note that he had placed a gun to his head, but had been coaxed out of it by police.

Then, she looked up at the top of the document to read his general details.

Name: Blake McPherson
Age: 40

Place of Residence: Los Angeles
Sex: Female

Chapter 7

Shockwaves were still reverberating through Faith's body as she drove Blake home. She kept staring at his crotch area but then once his eyes met hers, she averted her eyes.

Faith wanted to act as if everything was normal in front of him. Watching the news on her phone, she saw that a politician had gotten into an even bigger scandal and Blake's sex allegation scandal had been pushed to the backburner.

She drove the car as carefully as she could as if she was carrying the most sensitive load of her life. Faith hoped she wouldn't hit as much as a bump on her way home. Blake was still in a worrying state.

Once they arrived at their condo, Faith opened the car door for Blake. He took her hand and squeezed it as if trying to rely on her strength to get up. His hands grabbed her face and he kissed her as passionately as he had when they first met. His eyes gleamed as if the sun had turned them into emeralds from a fancy jewelry store.

"You know I love you, right?" Blake whispered.

"I know," Faith said with hesitation.

She hugged him but it felt like she was hugging a stranger. She didn't know who he was and she was deathly afraid to ask.

Faith and Blake slowly made their way to the elevator with Blake clutching her on the small of her back. She still loved the way he smelled, his rough hands, and his well moisturized beard. He was still a beautiful man.

She made Blake some soup and allowed him to

relax for the rest of the afternoon. He had changed into sweatpants and placed a wool comforter over himself. She attended to his needs as if he was a baby.

He smelled like a man. He walked like a man. He had a heavy, masculine voice. He even had a masculine sense of humor.

Faith refused to believe it. It was possible that the doctor had just checked the wrong box. She and Blake had had sex before. Most of the time it was oral sex, but lately, she had been pleasuring herself so she wouldn't have to bother him. Blake was either never home or too tired to have sex.

Blake continued watching TV until he fell asleep. She watched his toned chest rise up and down with his mouth wide open.

Faith sat across from him with her laptop open. Mary had invited her to a "Find Bianca" group online. She clicked "join" and then decided to write a message on their official website thanking everyone who had supported them thus far.

Blake had told her that he was coming up with an entirely different game plan. He was going to close the church and do online only. They would sell merchandise, make videos, sell books, and make special appearances for a fee. All their bad publicity was still publicity. Blake had fired his old team and was planning on hiring an all new group of experienced people for his new project.

Faith slipped her house shoes off and tip toed over to the sleeping Blake. The TV was still on, so she turned down the volume. She sat on a small section of the couch next to his chest. She slid her hands down his chest and then attempted to pull the band of sweatpants away from his skin. She then attempted to lift his boxer briefs but was met with a shocking slap of her hand that made her pull away in fear.

"What's wrong? I thought you were asleep," Faith said.

"Yeah, until I saw you trying to molest me."

"I can't look at my husband naked? What kind of marriage is this? Are you my brother?" Faith said trying to joke around.

Blake pushed her off and she fell to the floor.

"I don't like being touched like that. I'm not hard. You don't touch a man right there when he's soft."

"I'm sorry. I won't do it again. Let's change the subject. Did you want to start planning out our virtual Sundays now? What are we going to do about the building we purchased?"

"I'm thinking about making that a partial warehouse for our merchandise. I'll figure it out. Right now, my main thing is to do what I can with as little help as possible."

It made Faith tingle a little when he spoke about making moves. He was a resilient man that didn't let anything hold him down for too long.

He was prescribed psychiatric medication because the doctor had diagnosed him with Bipolar Disorder. Faith was glad he was taking medication because it would probably make him less aggressive.

Over the next few days, Faith noticed that Blake's romantic interest had begun to die down. He was on his computer all day long and only left to go to his studio to record videos. His sermons were going viral again and money from their T-shirts, personalized Bibles, and books began to come in. Faith knew things were looking up when she saw that he had one of the top trending videos on a popular Christian website.

Although Blake had told her not to, she had still

decided to keep in contact with Mary. Faith hoped that she would eventually run into Bianca at the grocery store, the gym, or one of the popular outdoor malls. Everywhere she went, she kept an eye out for the green eyed, wavy haired girl with the playful smile.

Blake and Cameron decided to work with each other again so, on Saturday night, Faith was home alone once again.

She passed by his video recording studio, and saw that his laptop was still open. Without trying to fight her curiosity, she sat in his office chair and looked through his tabs.

His email was still open. As she carefully went read the title of each email, nothing seemed off. She looked around and then decided to look at his website history.

He had visited numerous gay and lesbian websites. They weren't pornographic but to socialize and find common interests. She couldn't find any messages from him but she did see searches for hormone injections. He searched for video production techniques and had viewed old articles in defense of him concerning the sexual abuse scandal.

His email was open on another tab. Her heart was pounding in her chest because she knew he could arrive at any time. She saw that it was for a dating website for Christian singles. He had been talking to both men and women trying to meet them.

Faith grew more furious with each message she read. He had much more interaction with women and had apparently met up with a few of them. He told at least five women that he was single and looking. He had confessed to a woman that looked less than half his age that he and his wife were going through a divorce. The woman had recognized him and wanted to know why he was on a dating site if he was married.

Large drops of tears fell from her eyes onto the keyboard in front of her. She didn't even care if she short circuited his laptop. She wanted to spill water all over it and then throw it outside. She thought about keying his car and even throwing his clothes out.

Once she caught her breath, Faith thought it would be best to keep her composure once he walked in. She would have a normal conversation with him and then start asking the real questions.

His text messages had been linked to his computer. She saw one pop up. It was from Cameron.

Hey, Daddy. Just thinking about you. You home?

Faith almost sunk to the floor when she began to read their conversations. They had been talking faithfully for the last two months. Ever since Blake lost Vision Spiritual Center, they had grown closer.

Blake had always been upset when she assumed that she was talking to Cameron. Although Cameron was handsome, she never felt as if she wanted to leave her husband and everything they built for him.

What she read almost made her sick to her stomach. Blake, Cameron, and Jessie Madison used to have threesomes. The times when she thought he was going on a work trip, he had been visiting Cameron in secret. Faith thought Jessie Madison was a lesbian so she wondered how she would have had any interest in Blake. The group message thread between Blake, Cameron, and Jessie Madison were making her head hurt. It appeared as if Blake had promised her a big cut of the African Charity money and he took back his promise at the last minute. He had also promised to make her his assistant pastor but eventually took back that promise too. It appeared as if that was what led Jessie Madison to take down her husband's church and accuse him of assault.

Faith had pushed away everyone who had been in

her corner such as Tara and her mother. She had no one to lean on as he had made her believe that everyone was against their marriage and faith. Unfortunately, Blake had been the only one working against her since they said their "I Dos."

Her female intuition was still bothering her. Blake had to be hiding something else from her. She didn't know if it was money, sexually transmitted diseases, or even his name. He had been so secretive that all she knew about him was what he wanted her to know.

A text from him made her jump.

I'm on my way. Wyd?

Faith wanted to squeeze her phone so tightly she wished it could have shattered into her hand. The blood that would have resulted wouldn't have been able to match all the pain she felt.

Nothing. I'm just waiting on you to come home.

Faith put on a comfortable Nike sweat suit and put her fluffiest socks on her feet. She wanted to play soft music in the background but she hated playing music while her nerves were shaky.

A few times she thought she might have to vomit before he came into the door. She slowly sipped peppermint tea while she stared at the front door. Her right leg shook violently.

Ten minutes later, Faith heard Blake's key enter the door. She placed her teacup down and managed to force a smile.

"What you sitting here for?" Blake asked.

"I was just relaxing."

She watched him look around and sniff. Their dog ran up to him from their bedroom and lied on her back to be rubbed.

"You didn't cook?" He said with one eyebrow raised. He was wearing a dark blue collared shirt with a golden cross gently laying on his chest. He loosened his *Ferragamo* belt and tossed onto the lounge chair closest to him. Faith felt her body flinch the moment the belt left his hand.

"No. I didn't. Not this time."

"Okay? So, what am I going to eat?"
"You can eat all those texts you sent Cameron and Jessie Madison."

Faith felt as if every decibel of sound across the world stopped. Their window was open so she usually heard a few sounds of the cars, birds, and people on the sidewalk.

There was nothing.

If she listened closely, she swore the blood in her

veins sounded like a raging waterfall.

"What?"

Blake tilted his head and took one step backward. He then shook his head and went into the nest room to change into basketball shorts and a white t-shirt.

He came back into the room but the boiling of her blood had yet to cease.

"You heard me. You left your laptop open."

Faith kept her eyes locked in on Blake's. It was a stare down like two lions on the savannah competing for dominance.

Suddenly, her beating heart transitioned from feelings of wanting to run away like a scared rabbit into a desire to charge toward her opponent.

"Are you serious right now?" Blake said with his fists clenched.

"You've been seeing Cameron and Jessie Madison. You've been going on dating sites. I took screenshots and saved them in my email. You've been cheating this whole time!"

Faith wanted to burst into tears but she took a deep breath to help keep her composure.

"And what are you going to do about it?" Blake said, biting his bottom lip. "What was I supposed to do with a boring ass wife?"

"You barely, if ever, had sex with me! You avoided me! Were you even attracted to me in the first place? Was I just being used this whole time?"

Faith thought Blake's fists were going to come toward her but instead he crossed his arms. His chest protruded forward and his green eyes narrowed on her. It was almost as if their color had darkened in an instant.

"You wanted to live this life. You wanted it all. I gave it all to you. The purses. The cars. The vacations. The jewelry. You wouldn't be able to do any better. You were an office assistant when I met you. You were working at school. You could barely afford the little apartment you had. I upgraded your whole life. You mean to tell me you're gonna try and leave me?"

Blake began to laugh so hard he bent down at the waist. "You really think you're gonna do better than me? You're not that cute."

Faith felt his words cut through her chest like a million needles. Still, she wouldn't let a single tear escape her eye.

"I refuse to let this life we've built together keep me from having a single strand of dignity. I don't have to

237

live with a man who doesn't love me."

"Yes, but you'll live with me. You'll deal with it. Where are you going to go? You'll be living in a box by the time the ink on the divorce papers are signed. I know people. Yes, this is a community property state but you'll be trying to get out of town by the time I'm finished with you."

"Is that a threat? I'm entitled to half of everything. You can't take anything away from me. But I rather leave this marriage dirt poor than deal with you cheating on me left and right."

"As if *you* haven't?"

"I haven't! I stayed faithful to you! I would never do something like that! You never wanted kids and you were always out doing whatever. I cooked and cleaned. I stood by your side during this whole sex allegation fiasco only to find out you and Miss Madison had been seeing each other."

"You won't leave. You say that but you won't," Blake arrogantly shrugged his shoulders and gave her a half smile.

Blake slid past Faith and attempted to take his seat on the couch. His shirt slightly lifted and Faith saw a strange piece of plastic gripping his lower body near his pelvis. He was slightly hard so she could see the penis imprint through his basketball shorts.

Rage overcame her and she charged toward him. All Faith could see was red.

It seemed like everything around her had resulted in slow motion.

She watched him slowly face her before he took his seat. Faith pulled his basketball shorts down to his ankles.

He attempted to cover it but it was too late. She couldn't believe that he was wearing a silicone penis on an obvious vagina.

"A strap on?"

"It's a prosthetic because I got into an accident."

"No, it's not," Faith said calmly. "Who are you, Blake?"

"I'm your husband."

"No, apparently you're my wife. Are you a woman?"

"I...am not."
"Are you Bianca?"

She watched Blake begin to break out in tears.

"Is this why you supposedly have no family?"

"I thought no one would love me! How would I ever find love? You loved me for me and now all of a sudden you don't? You took that vow before God and now you're going to throw me away like trash?"

Faith tried to pull her legs away from his arms that were clutching her with so much pressure she felt her knees buckle.

She released herself from her grip and ran upstairs to grab her cellphone, purse, and laptop. She put a jacket on and tied her hair up in a bun.

"You leave and I'm changing the locks," Blake said fiercely.

"That's a risk I'm willing to take." She could feel her voice shaking and part of her didn't want to leave the comfort of the only home she knew.

Faith heard him bolt the door and she ran down the stairs instead of waiting on the elevator. She got in her car and opened her texts so she could find Mary's number.

Her hands were shaking so violently, she could barely put the phone up to her ear as she hadn't even started the car yet.

"Hello? Mary? This is Faith. I found your daughter."

❖

Faith relished the warmth from Tara rubbing her back. She had her head in hands. Her right leg shook and her stomach kept churning.

"I knew something was wrong with that man or I mean woman," Tara sighed. "Don't worry. She's gonna get hers. All this will come out."

"I kind of don't want it to because then everybody is going to judge me. People aren't going to be able to believe that I was mistakenly married to a woman. I'll look like a complete idiot."

"Don't worry about how you'll look. Just worry about getting better and getting away from that disgusting person. They did you wrong. Don't sit here and blame yourself."

"Blake's mother is on the way to California. She was jumping up and down when I told her the news. I sent her the pictures of him and she said that she knows her child's eyes. She also recognized the smallest cut above his eyebrow. She said Bianca fell onto a glass table when she was two years old."

"We're gonna get some answers. This is a mess beyond belief. I'm just glad you're out of that cult. When was even the last time you read your Bible?"

"I haven't been able to do anything but sit up under Blake and sit pretty. I had no identity of my own. He took everything away from me. I feel so used."

Faith allowed Tara to pull her in so she could cry freely. It took hours to console her. Unfortunately, Tara's apartment was her home now since she had nowhere to go. Blake had been sending her threatening texts all evening. Tara demanded that she turn her phone off.

Faith had been successfully able to refrain from having any contact with Blake. She had unblocked his number but her email inbox was filled with his threats.

She had been living with Tara for the past week who made sure she had clothes and food available. Faith couldn't believe she had a friend who would extend such hospitality to her. She felt like she didn't deserve it but she had no choice. Her mother had recently sold her home and moved to Texas. Faith still wasn't ready to admit to her mother what happened. At least Tara hadn't said "I told you so" so many times until it sickened her.

On a gray Friday afternoon, Faith felt feelings of depression hit her like heavy bricks. She had gone into her bank account and it had been cleaned out. She had pawned the jewelry she had worn when she left including her engagement ring but she knew that money would run out soon.

Tara had just come home from work and Faith heard her footsteps but she refused to look over her shoulder. Tears were beginning to well up in her eyes again.

"Girl, are you on social media like I told you not to? It's not good for your mental health."

"Tara, he cleaned out our bank account. I don't have anything."

"You still calling Blake a 'he?'" Tara said with a slight laugh. "You need to secure a lawyer. I'll help you.

We're gonna get her ass good. Don't worry. She owes you half."

"I just want to reapply for the same job I have and get my life back in order. I'm tired of living with this void. I feel relieved that he's gone but it's like my whole fairytale was just ripped like a rug from underneath my feet. I feel like I'm still slipping."

"You call that a fairytale?" Tara said, filling up a glass of water. She pulled a stool out in front of Faith and attempted to lift her chin. "That was never a fairytale, Faith. You were living in a nightmare. All that was a fantasy. You better thank God that he's finally bringing you out of it and has opened your eyes. Thankfully you didn't, or rather you couldn't, have kids with Blake. Then, you'd be really locked in. That man was cheating left and right, making you look like the fool. I'll tell you one thing, though, you'll be the last one laughing all the way to the bank."

Faith was still sniffling and drank a glass of water.

"Faith, this is the time for you to pray, reflect, and take care of yourself. Use a different email. Block him on everything and contact a lawyer. That's how we'll take this demon down."

Faith was eventually left alone to watch TV. She turned on the movie *Waiting to Exhale* and brewed a cup of tea.

She admitted that sitting on Tara's couch was the most relaxed she had felt in a long time. She felt like she was on edge in her own home all the time. Her heart no longer anxiously skipped a beat when she heard noises from outside or when the front door opened. For a long time she felt like she was a prisoner in her own home but that had become her "normal."

Before Blake, her life had revolved around Jesus but, during their marriage, her life centered around Blake.

She had been married to a pastor but ended up worshipping money, obsessed with being married to a handsome man, and focused on taking hold of power in the church.

Her eyes were beginning to close. She felt a wave of tiredness. She then felt her phone vibrating on the couch.

It was Mary.

"Hello?" Faith began.

"I'll just make this quick. I'm on my way to California. I got a last minute ticket. Can you text me Bianca's address?"

"You're going to visit Blake?"

"I am. This might be my only chance. Financially, I haven't been doing that well. I just got laid off but I had some money saved up and all I want to do is see my baby. The Lord told me that my child wasn't dead. I can't wait to see her.”

Faith sent Mary her old address where she assumed Blake still lived. She even gave her directions on how to easily get up to their penthouse.

“I hope you two have a wonderful meeting. I won’t be there, though. I live with a friend of mine to get back on my feet. I’m trying to begin divorce proceedings.”

“I don’t blame you. She did all this lying trying to force someone to be a lesbian. I know she not gonna wanna see me, but I’m her momma. I birthed that child.”

“Yes, Ma’am. Well I’ll send you the information right now.”

Faith texted Mary and then sunk deeper into her position on the couch. She closed her eyes and began to tune the movie out but when she opened them again, the scene where Angela Bassett burns her husband’s belongings appears on the screen. That scene had never felt so powerful to Faith before.

She let one more tear of sadness fall from her eye. Internally, she promised herself that she would cry no more tears of hopelessness. All her crying from now on would be only war cries. Faith was positive that she would prevail on the other side. God hadn't let her down before so why would he do so now?

Faith had gotten back in contact with Mary after receiving a text about her arrival. She had been feeling calmer within the last twenty-four hours. Tara's couch bed felt so much more comfortable than the California King she shared with Blake during her tumultuous marriage.

I found her. She wanted to act like she didn't know who I was. God is so good!

I'm glad. Faith texted.

"Where you headed today?" Tara asked as she turned the T.V. on to check the weather.

"I think I'm just going to lay low again and fill out these applications. I might go to the store to buy some more peppermint tea for you. I think I made your last bag last night."

"Oh girl, you don't have to replace my stuff."

"No, I need to get some fresh air. I got to get out in the public and take my mind off things."

"Well suit yourself. I'll be back this evening."

Faith sunk deeper into her bed and then abruptly opened her eyes once she heard the opening theme for the morning news.

A bold headline read: **Former Spiritual Leader Charged with Charity Fraud**

Blake's picture flashed across the screen. Faith clutched her pillow behind her and prayed that they wouldn't show her picture too.

They didn't.

It had been discovered that Blake had been funneling the money that he had promised to charities into his personal accounts. The countries that he had promised money had still been reeling from natural disasters such as earthquakes and floods. People from Haiti were still recovering from the devastating earthquake that had destroyed more than seventy-five percent of the island. He had promised to give them one point three million dollars to help with food, shelter, and the rebuilding of schools.

The news segment claimed that all that money and more had been linked directly to private accounts. He had purchased a jet that was still on its way from Sweden as well as a luxury helicopter. They also found out that he had money in illegal foreign bank accounts so he wouldn't have to pay taxes to the country he was purchasing his items in.

They listed several other items he had splurged on that Faith hadn't even known about. What almost made her want to throw the TV out the window was when they claimed that he had used the church's funds to purchase a cottage or love den for his partner in crime, Cameron.

A picture of Blake and Faith flashed across the screen. Thankfully, she was not included in the exposé which was limited to what he had he had done on his own. Blake had been "kind" enough to write out personal checks and conduct business in his name only.

It was implied that she had benefited from Blake's schemes, but there was more information on Cameron and Jessie Madison.

Faith began searching for a lawyer to represent her at that moment. She opened her laptop and called a Beverly Hills law office. She explained her situation and they agreed to represent her right away.

Due to her high profile case and the potential of a media circus surrounding the scandal, Faith knew she would get the best attorney the law office could find. She might even be redirected to a famed celebrity attorney. All Faith wanted was to protect her interests and get the appropriate amount of money she was owed when she officially filed for divorce.

An hour later, before Faith planned to leave for the day, the lawyer, Sandra Mason from Mason, Jackson, and McGrath law in Beverly Hills called her.

Faith picked up the phone on the first ring. The lawyer asked if she wanted to be represented for a media interview. At first, Faith didn't want her face blasted on TV, but she wanted to clear her name of any wrongdoing. People, if they hadn't already, would begin to associate her with Blake's crimes. As his wife, she would have had to be complicit in his crimes. Doing a TV interview with her lawyer present and Blake absent would be the best way to start the process of clearing her name.

"I want to do it. I want you to work for me," Faith said confidently. "The media has to know that this person is a fraud. There are so many layers to them. I'll just tell you this before we get down to other business, Blake McPherson completely lied about their identity. Miss Mason, I have no idea who I married."

Feeling accomplished, Faith finally headed to the grocery store that evening. There was a sweet lemon cake that she enjoyed purchasing at the bakery next to Whole Foods. She put her jacket on and took the keys to the Black Tesla which was one of the only luxury items she had been able to take with her. Faith missed her dog the most but vowed to get her back after the divorce was finalized. She didn't want to live the life she lived before. She just craved normalcy again.

The underground parking lot was empty. Most people were still at work so Faith parked her car close to the handicap spots so she could get in and out.

She checked her surroundings and then grabbed her purse. Once she opened her car door, she spotted a black Tesla speeding inside as if it had been waiting there. She had seen a car behind her but thought nothing of it.

The car had its headlights on and swerved over to where Faith was standing.

Once she saw his eyes, she threw her purse back in the car and rushed to put her seatbelt back on. The next thing she saw was a gun pointing at her from the passenger side window.

"Get the fuck out."

Chapter 8

Faith remained in her car and started her engine to back up. She was sure that Blake was either drunk or high because his eyes were bugged out. He was in a tank top with sweat dripping down his body.

He stepped out of his car while Faith was backing up. She attempted to back up but Blake jumped in front of her with his gun pointing in her direction.

"Get out of the damn car, bitch!"

Faith's hands shook and the sweat from her palms almost made them slip off the steering wheel.

Faith attempted to drive in the other direction but Blake got in front of her again.

"I'm gonna kill you. You won't take anything from me!"

Faith wanted to shout as loudly as she could about how he was a fraud but she held her tongue and attempted to reach for her purse to call the police. Her arm stretched to the passenger seat to slide her phone out of her purse.

Once she did that, he pulled the trigger and shot into the headrest of her passenger seat. Faith screamed and attempted to drive her cat around him but, with the gun in his hand, he was able to get in front of her car once again.

This time, Faith knew that it was either him or her. She was going to have to figure out how to survive this and quickly.

She backed her car up and Blake took two steps backward.

"Once I pull this shit, I don't care if I go to jail. I'm

going to prison anyway."

He pulled the trigger and shot at her passenger side tire but it hit the rim. Taking a deep breath, Faith pushed her foot on her gas pedal as heavy as she could. Her Tesla picked up speed much faster than she thought and Blake's body launched into the air. Faith kept driving until she met the entrance of the garage.

The gun in his hand ended up at least twenty feet away from him. The police sirens began to approach her. She was glad someone had been able to call the police.

Once Faith exited her car, she had glass on her lap and her hands were still shaking. She stared at Blake from afar hoping he would get up.

Within seconds, the ambulance arrived and it seemed as if all at once, it was a buzzing scene out of a movie. The emergency responders began doing CPR on Blake. Faith moved closer toward him but a policeman stopped in front of her to question her.

"Sir, he is my estranged husband. He shot at me. I shot at my car twice. I rammed my car into him to get away. I'm so sorry, I didn't know what to do."

Faith began to break down once she watched the paramedics continue to try to save Blake's life with an oxygen mask. They continued pumping his chest but she saw that his eyes were still closed.

"I'm so sorry, officer. I'm so sorry," she continued to gasp.

"Ma'am, we'll just take you in for questioning. We need to know more."

She saw the police inspecting the damage to her car and furiously write in her notebook.

"I'll go," she said.

Blake's death had sent shockwaves through the Christian community. However, the way he died was eventually overshadowed by the fact that now everyone knew he had been living as a man but born a woman.

Many people that he had worked with were angry that he had stolen from charities and misrepresented himself. Public opinion of Faith soon went from anger to compassion within a few days. Before her court date, she had been able to have a televised interview with Oprah talking about her abuse and how she didn't know she was married to a woman.

To her surprise, there had been an outpour of love from all over the nation. Although Faith was willing to take the blame and do time for killing her former husband, public opinion swayed in her favor. Faith still had abusive emails and even marks on her body from what he had done to her.

The only person Faith was afraid of was his mother. She had just gotten the opportunity to reconnect with Blake and she had taken that away.

Faith decided to still live with Tara for moral support because she was afraid to be on her own. The thought of having killed someone weighed on her conscience every day but Tara reassured her daily that it wasn't her fault.

"Girl, anyone with a gun in their face would have done the same thing." Tara said while she and Faith sat on the couch watching a romance comedy.

"I know but I didn't have to kill him. I didn't mean to kill. I don't feel that God will ever forgive me."

"God will forgive you for trying to save your own life while you had the barrel of a gun in your face."

Faith allowed a single tear to fall. She was feeling

better each day but she knew it would weigh on her heart forever.

"You wanted to be free, Faith. God is now giving you the chance to be your own woman and live the beautiful life you always dreamed of. Someday, you'll see this as a blessing."

Faith could hear her phone buzzing from the coffee table. She saw it was a call from Mary, Blake's mother.

"It's Mary, what do I do?"

"You don't have to answer it."

"I just want to know what she might say. I need closure. If she hates me then she hates me but I need to close this chapter."

Tara shrugged her shoulder and took a sip of her coffee. "Let the Lord lead you."

"Hello?" Faith answered the phone before she feared it would stop ringing.

"Faith? It's Mary."

"Yes. How are you doing?"

"I'm well. How are you?"

Faith began sobbing uncontrollably. The tears from her eyes began to make the phone slip off her face. She could barely breathe until Tara located a box of tissues.

"Why are you crying so hard?" Mary asked. Faith could barely hear her because the phone was off her ear.

"I killed your daughter. I'm so sorry. I'm just so sorry. I know I will never be able to bring her back but…"

Mary cut her off. "Faith, realistically, she had killed you before you ever did anything to her. I read and heard what Bianca did to you. I simply don't know what kind of person she became after she left me and disappeared. She lied to you, she lied to me, and she lied to the church. She didn't lie to God though. He knew who she was. But, Sweetheart, I didn't know who Bianca became once she left to go to California. I spoke to her for a little bit sometime before she died and, apparently, I did nothing for them and they hated me. All I could do was pray for their soul. I'm sorry she did what she did to you. But, Faith, don't feel bad for me. I've accepted all that has happened and I forgive you."

Faith cried so hard, no sound would leave her mouth. She attempted to calm her body down and took a few deep breaths. "Thank you, Mary. Thank you. I appreciate it."

"And I'll make sure I stand up for you in court. I know the courts are going to try to throw the book at you but we got to stay prayerful."

"We will," Faith said hoarsely.

After she ended the call, Tara left the room to give Faith time to process.

Faith took a few deep breaths and took a few sips of water. The TV was turned off, and all she could hear was the faint chirping of birds outside and a few cars driving by. She focused on the silence for a while and closed her eyes to pray.

It felt like a massive weight had been lifted off her shoulders once Mary had forgiven her. The media was beginning to look at her like a hero for being the abused woman who got away. Blake had a trail of evil following his memory and most of it had not been attached to her name. She had been given access to the accounts that Blake had locked. She had begun to list the charities that she would be giving the money to. She wanted to keep nothing and start all over. She knew many people would think she was crazy not to live in luxury after everything that happened but Faith knew in good conscience she could not live the rest of her life knowing that her money was from forming fake charities.

An hour later, Faith noticed that Tara was gone. She picked up her phone and thought to call her lawyer to discuss their game plan. She wanted the truth to come out to the jury. Her main goal was so that no one thought she was complicit in what Blake had done.

After speaking with her lawyer, she went on social media again. Tara and her mother had told her to take a social media break. Faith knew it was going to be too difficult to stay away too long. She wanted to know if people were still talking about her situation and what they thought. She had become obsessive about it.

The church's website and social media pages had been defunct for a while. Faith had deactivated her account that was linked to many church officials and former members. This time, she planned on using a personal account that she hadn't touched since she quit being an administrative assistant.

However, after just fifteen minutes scrolling down her phone, she had become saddened by much more than the scandal she was caught in ever could.

Many of her former friends, relatives, and acquaintances had moved on to marry and have children. They had bought homes together and gone on trips. Their children took their first steps, said their first words, and began their first school days.

Faith's heart had never hurt so much before. Blake had taken away more than her sense of peace. He knew she wanted children and could not give that to her. At forty-years old, Faith was beginning to fear it was too late. Had she missed the bus forever?

Her greatest envy was of a woman she used to follow when she was still working for the school district. She had quit her job to be a missionary overseas. Instead of just giving to a charity, she *was* the charity. Chasing love from a man who didn't love her back had done severe damage to her relationship with God. Thankfully, it was reversible. She had turned her back on God but he hadn't turned his back on her.

It was going to take one day at a time with prayer and meditation to get back to where she was. Faith knew she hadn't been genuinely happy for a long time. The things that Blake gave her made her happy for a short period of time but she had lost all her joy for life. Life had just become about chasing things and trying hard to stay by the side of one of the most handsome men in the church circuit of Southern California. He was a celebrity preacher and she wanted to be his celebrity wife.

When she was with him, people listened to her. She was no longer just the average Black woman walking down the street. She had a name. She was Mrs. McPherson.

As of now, she was just Faith and Faith was going to have to rediscover who she was before it was too late.

❖

Faith didn't think she could thank God enough when she was found "Not Guilty" by the jury. Since she had outlined her abuse and how she attempted to get away from him in the parking lot several times, the court did not believe that she was a cold-blooded killer.

Mary had come to each court hearing to support her and it gave Faith great joy to know that she had so many women on her side. Her mother, Tara, and even her former coworkers supported her.

After hearing the verdict, Faith cried and hugged her lawyer. She knew that the interviews and book deals would line up right away. She would be able to make money off this and go back to living her own life. It would be possible for her to purchase an apartment or home. It wouldn't even be necessary for her to get back to work immediately.

Faith had given most of her money away but she still had enough to live comfortably for the next few months.

Once Faith exited the courtroom, her mother hugged her so tightly she could barely breathe.

"God is so good. I had been praying you leave that man. I had been praying. I think it would happen like this but I had been praying for God to bring you out. I didn't like who you had become. I know my daughter. I know my child. I know what you're capable of and you're no crook. The Lord gave you a second chance."

"He did and I'm going to have to use it wisely."

Her lawyer motioned for her to come outside the courtroom to interview. Faith took her mother's hand and then went in her direction.

"I'll do just this one. But, I don't think I'll be doing

any more."

"But Honey, You have so much opportunity now. Everyone wants to talk to you."

"That's the problem. I let everybody talk to me but God."

Faith looked at her mother. "I let everyone talk to me except those that mattered the most."

Faith went outside to take questions by different news outlets. She was bombarded with a variety of questions such as how she managed to escape Blake and when she found out he was having extramarital affairs. Her lawyer recommended that she not answer any personal questions about the details of her marriage and the killing.

She obeyed and limited the amount of questions for what she could answer in less than ten minutes.

After she left the journalists and news cameras,

Faith and her mother took a black town car back to Tara's apartment where she still lived.

"You gonna move out soon?" Her mother asked.

"I am but I'm not planning on getting an apartment or house or anything."

"What are you going to do?" Her mother's eyebrows raised.

"I'm going to do what I always wanted to do. I'm not going to let life pass me by. God is too good."

"You're going to travel?"

"Somewhat. I have plans on what I'm going to do. I just got several interview requests from different jobs. I got a call back from the school district too. They want me to work downtown. It would be more of a "cushy" job instead of working directly in the schools."

"You're gonna take it right?"

"No. I'm not."

Three minutes of silence was shared between them after Faith responded. Her mother shrugged her shoulders and shook her head. She knew her mother tended to live in more anxiety than she did and thrived off plans, she would be asking more questions about her potential occupation for the foreseeable future.

"I know this whole thing maybe probably makes you want to put off marriage for a while but I want you to know that all men aren't like Blake."

"Well, Blake wasn't a man, Mother," Faith chuckled.

"You know what I mean. I don't want you to not ever seek having a husband and kids ever again. I know you want a family, right?"

Faith crossed her arms and stared out the window as their car dragged through midday Downtown Los Angeles traffic.

"Mother, I've learned that having a man doesn't complete me. I don't need a husband to be happy. I needed to find happiness in myself first. That's what I was lacking. I thought Blake made me happy. He just allowed me to be satisfied with the few luxury items he gave me. I wasn't truly happy but now I know what does make me happy. I've been praying and I believe that God has sent me the answer."

"The Lord doesn't want you to give up on having someone, Faith."

"Mother, you named me 'Faith.' Right now, you're acting like you don't have any. I'm a woman in the middle of healing. The last thing I want to talk about right now is how I need to get married and rush to have children. I do want kids but I want them in a stable, loving environment.

Even if Blake hadn't lied to me about who he was, that was not the right environment to raise a child in. It just wasn't."

She watched her mother's shoulder's sink and her eyes began studying the ground.

"Then what do you plan on doing?"

"I'm going to do the missionary work that I've always wanted to do. I'm going to help abused women and hungry children around the world. I've joined a program to allow me to do just that. If my marriage had taught me anything, it's that there are women around the world who have suffered and are suffering just like me and didn't have the money nor the access to safety like I did. I want to help them. I've learned that it isn't about me. I've gotten out and if I could help one more woman get out, I've blessed somebody and that's my purpose in life. That is my God-given purpose."

"Then I believe in you. Be careful. I love you."

Faith and her mother remained silent for the rest of the ride. She kissed her mother "goodbye" when they arrived at the hotel she was staying at.

"I love you, Mother. Have a wonderful flight back. I'll talk to you later."

❖

Faith took a deep breath as she gazed over the Jamaican coastline from her patio. She closed her eyes and took in the roaring waves from the ocean in front of her.

She wasn't on vacation. This was her first week at the Wellington Home for Women and Children. The Christian-based refuge was for women who had been victims of domestic violence and had been trying to get away from their abusers. The women were housed, fed, and encouraged to find work to care for themselves. There was a missionary/counselor assigned to a group of women.

Almost instantly, many of the young women were drawn to her. She didn't know if it was because she was from America or because her stories about suffering abuse and lies from her former husband intrigued them.

One young lady, Natisha, who had a two-year-old daughter and golden brown skin asked several questions about why Faith wouldn't leave her abuser for such a long time.

"I wanted the status of being a wife. I wanted the money. I wanted to feel important. I didn't want people to know I had made a mistake."

Natisha's doe-like eyes had followed her every word as if she was a prophet coming to spread the word of God.

Most of the women that joined were either Christian or were raised Christian so the Wellington House didn't have to do a lot of converting.

Faith had room and board as well as a small

stipend. She had brought few belongings with her and agreed to help tend to the farmland that fed everyone.

Life was simpler, cleaner, and distant from the hustle and bustle of Downtown living. There was no room for showing off luxury watches and cars. She had no one that cared about the release of her newest book and "McPherson-Brand" Bible case.

Suddenly, she had been able to start anew. Her life now revolved around the needs of others. No longer did she think of what she wanted to do or wanted to look like. There were women and children who depended on her as a refuge when they were feeling lost and hurt.

Her job allowed her to lead prayer circles, teach new skills, and watch young children grow up to consider her their unofficial aunt or second mother.

She had limited her technology as well. She had a laptop but it was only for business. Faith had gone back to using a flip-phone just for calling. Her life no longer revolved around what other people thought of her. Jesus' love was not a quote she posted on her timeline. She was now expressing it every day.

It was Sunday morning and it was the only day of rest she got. Sundays were for church, to cook dinner, and play board games with the children who lived at The Wellington House. She took a warm shower since it was a hot day and slipped on a linen dress that she tied at her waist. She unwrapped her headscarf and let her long braids slip down to her waist.

Being in Jamaica, she didn't feel like she needed things in her possession all the time. A simple canvas bag and her Bible were all she needed on a regular day. She barely ever carried around credit cards because most of the places where she ate took cash, and she swore the food tasted better.

Faith entered the main lobby a few minutes after

getting dressed to meet the ladies who were ready to walk to church. Natisha was already dressed with her legs crossed at the knee. Once Faith and Natisha's eyes met, the young woman embraced her like a long lost sister.

"You down here already, Natisha?"

"I am."

"Just over here thinking? Let's get ready to go!" Faith said lifting her purse higher on her shoulder.

"Miss Faith, you are the strongest woman I know."

Faith chuckled.

"No, you really are. I don't know any women that walk around so happy to be independent. You don't have a boyfriend, husband, or children but you're so happy."

"Of course I am. Why wouldn't I?"

Natisha began to walk toward the door but her voice was still lowered.

"Miss Faith, most of the women I grew up around just put up with bad men in their life because they had no other choice. My own grandmother told me that it's no point in being alone. She said that as long as you have a man you're doing better than most other women."

Faith grabbed Natisha's hand and tried to stop the tears from bursting in her eyes. She knew right then why she had come to Jamaica. She had been able to find a way out but there were more women like Natisha who were being told the lie that a man was your only source of happiness.

"Natisha, I don't want to call your grandmother a liar but she was wrong about men. If a husband is what you desire, then go for it. I may want to get back on the horse one day myself but, right now, I thank God every day that some man who puts his hands on me is not my source of self-esteem."

Faith rested her finger on Natisha's chin. "Sweetheart, you are beautiful with or without a gentleman by your side. You're a beautiful woman and mother on the inside and out. But you're luckier than me. You're finding this out early. I learned my lesson a little later. The devil may send his false prophets but it is up to you to know when you've truly found true love. For some women that is difficult. But, Natisha, right here, right now, I've found my true happiness in helping girls like you see the strength that God already put within you."

"Thank you, Miss Faith," Natisha said softly.

"Are you ready to start our journey to church?"

"At this point, I'll follow you everywhere Miss Faith."

"To God be the glory," Faith gently chuckled. "To God be the glory."

To submit a manuscript to be

considered, email us at

submissions@majorkeypublishing.com

Be sure to LIKE our Major Key

Publishing page on Facebook!

CPSIA information can be obtained
at www.ICGtesting.com
Printed in the USA
LVHW041738011020
667692LV00004B/852

9 798653 055188